LIARS

No-one but you
knows the truth

For the real Jeremy Quay—thanks for the laughs!—Jack Heath

Scholastic Australia
An imprint of Scholastic Australia Pty Limited
PO Box 579 Gosford NSW 2250
ABN 11 000 614 577
www.scholastic.com.au

Part of the Scholastic Group
Sydney • Auckland • New York • Toronto • London • Mexico City
New Delhi • Hong Kong • Buenos Aires • Puerto Rico

Published by Scholastic Australia in 2019.

Additional illustrations. Cover: abandoned building photo by Jamison Riley on Unsplash; alley and trash photo by Jadon Barnes on Unsplash; blood stains © Oksana Mizina/Shutterstock.com; concrete floor © leolintang/Shutterstock.com; fire © polygraphus/Shutterstock.com; microphone © studiovin/Shutterstock.com; running man © istockphoto.com/PeteSherrard; standing man © Jevgenij Avin/Shutterstock.com. Internals: banner © istockphoto.com/Lava4images; frame © istockphoto.com/gn8; grunge border © Gordan/Shutterstock.com; map icon © ananaline/Shutterstock.com; smiley faces © cTermit/Shutterstock.com; sports © Luciano Cosmo/Shutterstock.com.

A catalogue record for this book is available from the National Library of Australia

ISBN: 978-1-74299-341-6

Typeset in Versailles LT.

Printed in China by Hang Tai Printing Company Limited.

This product is made of material from well-managed FSC®-certified forests, recycled material, and other controlled sources.

10 9 8 7 6 5 4 3 2 1 26 27 28 29 30 / 2

LIARS

THE SET-UP

JACK HEATH

A Scholastic Australia Book

KELTON

Kelton Creek
Bridge
(and underpass)
Train Station
Golf Course
Town Centre
(including police station, town hall, motel, video store)
Suburbs
(including houses of Jarli, Doug and Bess)
Hospital

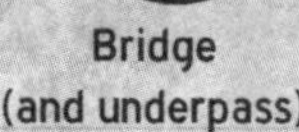

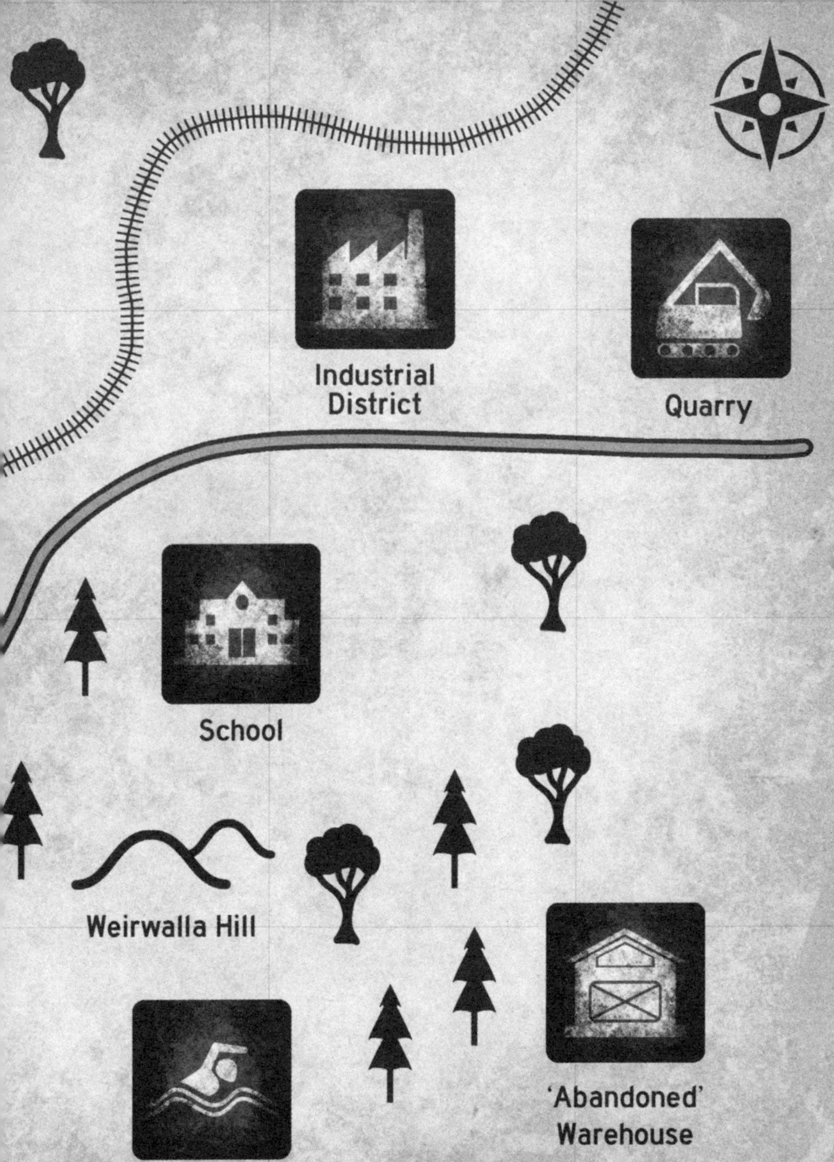
Industrial
District
Quarry
School
Weirwalla Hill
'Abandoned'
Warehouse
Lake

PART ONE: SKIRMISH

I THOUGHT GOOD PEOPLE WERE ALWAYS HONEST. NOW I KNOW THAT'S NOT TRUE. THE USAGE DATA FOR THE APP SUGGESTS THAT ALMOST EVERYBODY LIES. BUT GOOD PEOPLE DO IT TO PROTECT OTHERS. THEY SAY, 'LEAH'S NOT FEELING WELL', INSTEAD OF 'LEAH DOESN'T WANT TO TALK TO YOU'. BAD PEOPLE LIE ONLY TO PROTECT THEMSELVES. THEY SAY, 'LEAH'S NOT FEELING WELL', INSTEAD OF 'I POISONED HER'.

—From the documentation for Truth, *version 3.1*

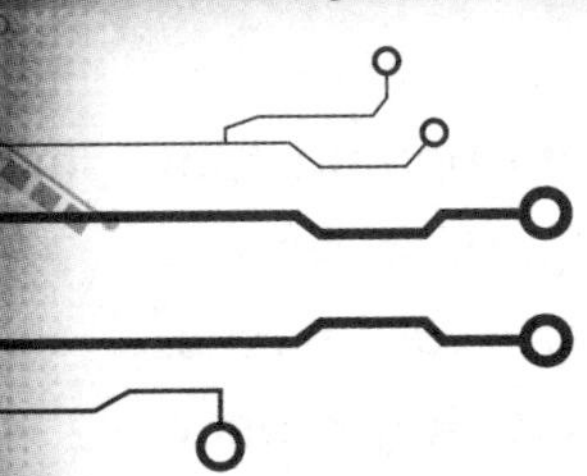

BATTLE OF THE BOTS

'I want to run the collision-detection script one more time,' Jarli said.

'We can't,' Doug insisted. 'We have to give them the robot in—' he checked his watch, 'fourteen minutes.'

'The test only takes eight minutes.'

'Yeah, but if you make any changes, you'll have to test it again. No time.'

Jarli chewed his nails. If his team won, he and Doug would each get a five-thousand-dollar government grant, and a mentorship with the famous tech guru Kellin Plowman. Jarli's dad had been in and out of hospital for months, unable to work. Mum had needed to take on a second job at the supermarket to cover the bills. Jarli thought the prize money would really help.

But if he and Doug lost, their humiliation would be very public. Hundreds of people were here.

Jarli's scalp prickled. He had the sudden sense that he was being watched.

He turned around. The long queue behind him was full of middle-aged nerds, teenagers staring at phones, fidgety children and exasperated parents. Some people looked—and smelled—like they'd been travelling all day to get here. No-one seemed to be looking at Jarli.

Maybe he was just picking up on the anxiety everyone else was feeling. Recently, people had reported seeing a figure roaming the streets of Kelton at night, face hidden by a red scarf with eyeholes cut into it. Some said it was a robber, although no-one seemed to have been robbed. Jarli's conspiracy-loving sister, Kirstie, said it was probably an alien who had escaped from a secret government lab. He had heard people refer to the figure as The Red Ninja. But Jarli doubted the figure even existed. Rumours quickly became exaggerated in a small town.

'Hey,' Doug said, watching Jarli. 'You OK?'

'What? Yeah. Fine.' Jarli took his eyes off the crowd. He didn't want to tell Doug what he'd felt. It was probably nothing. And Doug probably didn't need the extra stress.

Doug and his parents were in witness protection. They had changed their names and moved to Kelton to hide from a ruthless crime lord known only as VIPER. Three months ago, Viper had used contacts in the police force to find out Doug's new address, then crashed a plane into his house. Doug's family had barely survived. The police had offered them new identities, but they had turned them down. They didn't trust the authorities anymore.

The queue shuffled forwards. Jarli followed, one step closer to Kelton Town Hall. A banner hanging above the doorway read:

A smaller sign said:

ENTER AT YOUR OWN RISK.

Magnotech, Inc. *is not liable for injury.*

Doug clapped Jarli on the back. 'Don't look so jittery,' he said. 'Our robot is the best. We got this.'

They had reached the front door. Jarli could hear the rumbling of a crowd in the darkness beyond. Synth music boomed from hidden speakers.

'Tickets,' boomed a huge man in a black polo

shirt, his eyes hidden behind dark glasses.

'Tickets?' Jarli said, his voice suddenly squeaky. They hadn't been given tickets.

'No ticket, no entry,' the man said firmly. Veins bulged in his neck.

Jarli looked around for the rest of his class. But they had already gone inside. He and Doug had stayed back to do a last-minute oiling of the robot's wheels.

'We're not spectators,' Doug said quickly. 'We're competing.'

The huge man glanced at his phone. Jarli snuck a peek at the screen. The man was using *Truth Premium*—a rip-off of Jarli's own lie-detector app. It usually cost ninety-nine cents in the app store, but was currently on sale for free. Everyone seemed to have it now.

'We're competing,' Doug said again, louder.

The screen flashed green. **TRUE**

The doorman pocketed his phone. 'You boys are

late,' he said. 'And you're at the wrong entrance. Go around the side.'

He jerked a thumb to his left and turned to the next person in line. 'Tickets,' he said.

Doug and Jarli turned and hurried back past the queue, past the huge pillars and into the alley beside the town hall. A cold breeze tickled Jarli's hair. The bag bounced painfully against his hip. The robot inside was heavy, and the pincers at the front were sharp. Doug had named it 'Sir Ramington the fifth'—apparently there had been four previous models. None of them had ever made it to the competition stage.

'The email didn't say anything about a side entrance,' Jarli said, puffing.

Doug shrugged. 'I'm amazed there was an email at all. Pretty soon this town might actually join the twenty-first century.'

'Oi.' Jarli could make fun of Kelton because he and his family had lived here forever. But Doug had moved here only last year. It annoyed Jarli when Doug referred to his home town as 'the bum end of nowhere'.

The side entrance was an unmarked black door set into the stone wall, hidden by shadows. Jarli tried the handle. *Locked*. He knocked.

Doug checked his watch again. 'Eleven minutes.'

'What happens if we don't hand in our robot on time?' Jarli asked.

'Disqualified,' Doug said.

'Even if it's their fault for not telling us about the side entrance or not opening it when we get here?'

Keys rattled, and the door opened. A woman with dark hair in a tight bun appeared. She was wearing a headset microphone. Her lanyard read, STAGE MANAGER.

'You were supposed to be here at two-thirty,' she said, glaring at them. 'Is this your robot?'

Jarli held out the bag sheepishly. She snatched it from his hands.

'Careful,' Doug said.

'If it's fragile, it shouldn't be in the competition.' The stage manager walked away.

'Didn't even get the chance to say goodbye,' Doug said mournfully, only half-kidding.

Jarli caught the door just as it was about to fall shut. 'Are we supposed to follow her?'

'Guess so.'

They walked into the darkness and entered the backstage area. The door shut and locked itself behind them. The music was louder in here, thudding like a heartbeat. A screen hid the spectators from view, but Jarli could hear them muttering excitedly. Other competitors huddled in the corners, talking urgently in teams of four or five. They all looked older than Jarli and Doug. Jarli felt Sir Ramington's chances of winning slip away.

The stage manager reappeared. 'Listen up,' she shouted. 'Show starts in twenty minutes. Make sure you check the run-sheet over there so you know when you're on. There will be no victory speeches, and there will be no arguing with the judges. Win or lose, you get off the stage as soon as the winner is announced. Don't try to collect the pieces of your robot. They'll be collected by roadies.'

The muttering of the crowd behind the screen was slowly becoming a roar.

Jarli's phone dinged. Four messages from Jarli's best friend, Bess:

Have a bot of fun!

Break a meg(abyte).

Have you cyborganised an after-party?

Because you should, sooner rather than Vader.

Jarli wrote back:

Ha ha.

She replied:

I have more.

No, thanks. And BTW, Darth Vader isn't technically a robot.

He's not?

Jarli rolled his eyes.

I'll show you the movie tomorrow.

After you help me with my project. Right?

Whoops! I . . . didn't forget. I'll be there!

You better be. My mum will murder me if I fail science again. That's not a figure of speech—they'll find my body at the bottom of the lake next time it dries out.

Feeling guilty, Jarli walked over to the competition run sheet, which was stapled to a piece of plywood. There were only five match-ups. Sir Ramington was on first.

KELTON ROBATTLE™

1: Sir Ramington the Fifth vs Chloe

2: Terminizer vs Brobocop

3: Big Data vs Asimov Cocktail

4: Ice Borg vs Smashentennial Man

5: Bendertron vs Seanet

© & ™ Magnotech, Inc. All rights reserved. Robattle is a trademark of Magnotech Industries, Inc., a subsidiary of Plowman Enterprises, Inc.

Jarli nudged Doug. 'The order of the schedule is random, isn't it? They haven't put Sir Ramington on first because they think he's sure to lose . . . right?'

'Relax,' Doug said, reading over Jarli's shoulder. 'They wouldn't arrange the order based on—' He gasped.

'What's wrong?' Jarli asked.

'We're up against Chloe,' Doug stammered.

'Who's Chloe?'

'Chloe's a robot.'

'Well, duh. It's the Robattle.'

'My friend Rebecca was making a robot called Chloe.'

Doug whirled around suddenly and ducked behind Jarli. This didn't really work, since Jarli was smaller than him.

'Don't look,' Doug whispered, 'but Rebecca just walked in.'

'So what?' Jarli turned and spotted a teenage girl in a denim jacket wearing round Harry Potter-style glasses. She was looking around, carrying a bulky bag. Another competitor. She looked about Jarli's age, but Jarli didn't recognise her from school.

'I told you not to look!' Doug hissed.

Jarli turned back to Doug. 'I don't know her.'

'You don't get it,' Doug said. 'She was my friend *before*.'

Jarli's mouth fell open. Rebecca must be from Doug's old life, before he went into witness protection and moved to Kelton. If she saw him here, she could connect his old identity to his new one.

'Go that way,' Doug said, pointing to the bathroom. 'Go!'

Keeping himself between Doug and Rebecca, Jarli followed Doug to the bathroom and closed the door. It was a cramped space, designed only for one person. The floor was damp, and Jarli had to duck to avoid bumping his head on a coat hook.

'Maybe she won't recognise you,' Jarli whispered.

'We were best friends for a decade. She'll recognise me. What do we do?'

Jarli felt a sudden pang of sympathy for Doug. He imagined having to change his name and leave Bess behind. It hurt even to think about it.

'Doesn't Viper already know about your new identity?' Jarli said. 'So—'

'Yeah, but the rest of the world doesn't,' Doug said. 'The police reckon Viper hasn't attacked my family again because he doesn't think we're a threat anymore. So we've been keeping our heads down. If anyone works out who we really are, word will spread fast. We could be exposed online, then in newspapers, then on TV. Once we become the centre of attention, who says Viper won't change his mind about us?'

Jarli flashed back to a conversation with Scanner, a police officer who was undercover in Viper's gang. Scanner had warned Jarli to avoid attracting attention. It had sounded almost like a threat.

'We'll have to pull out of the competition,' Jarli

said. It would be awful to miss out on their chance to win the prize money and see how the robot performed in a real battle. But Doug's safety was more important.

'We can't,' Doug said. 'Not without calling even more attention to ourselves.'

'Sir Ramington!' The stage manager's voice echoed through the backstage area. 'Where is Sir Ramington's team?'

Jarli and Doug looked at each other.

'Rebecca and I will be on the stage,' Jarli said quickly. 'You can leave the building while she's distracted. OK?'

Doug nodded.

'Sir Ramington!' the stage manager yelled again.

'I'm coming!' Jarli called. With a last anxious glance at Doug, he slipped out the door.

The stage manager glared at Jarli as he approached. 'Where's your teammate?'

'Uh, he's sick,' Jarli said. 'He had to go home.'

The woman's phone beeped. LIE

Jarli recognised the sound. Her phone was running *Truth Premium*.

'OK,' Jarli admitted, 'he's in the bathroom. He's too scared to come out.'

This was technically true, and the woman's phone didn't react.

She rolled her eyes. 'Fine,' she said. 'Your match is cancelled.'

'What? No!' Jarli needed the match to go ahead, to distract Rebecca. Otherwise there would be no cover for Doug.

A man in a pale blue suit appeared from behind the screen. Even in the darkness of backstage he was wearing a white full-brim hat with a black band. 'Where is Sir Ramington's team?' he demanded.

Jarli gasped. This was Kellin Plowman—the rich benefactor of the competition. Jarli had admired him and his work for years. Plowman had invented an encryption that had become the basis for a cryptocurrency, making him a multimillionaire. His artificial-intelligence algorithms were used in hundreds of video games. He lived on an exclusive compound just outside of Kelton, where he built drones which sometimes won international competitions.

But he was also the owner of Magnotech, a hardware giant. Magnotech had recently been caught manufacturing weapons for Viper. There was no proof that Plowman had known anything about that, but the connection made Jarli cautious.

'One team member is—' the stage manager began.

'Right here,' Jarli said quickly. 'I'm ready to go on, Mr Plowman. Sir.'

Plowman looked Jarli up and down with steely grey eyes. ‘Where's your partner?’ he asked.

‘Don't need him,’ Jarli said. ‘I can go on by myself.’

‘You're the pilot?’

‘There is no pilot. The robot is autonomous.’

Most people were impressed when Jarli said this, but Plowman and the stage manager both knew enough about robotics to look doubtful instead.

‘Please,’ Jarli said. ‘Let me compete.’

Plowman scratched his beard. ‘Wait. Are you Jarli Durras? The one who made the app?’

Jarli swallowed. ‘You've heard of me?’

In retrospect, it was a silly question. Jarli's app hadn't made him rich, but it had made him famous. Everyone in Kelton had heard of him. Most of them had been busted by his app at least once.

Plowman exchanged a glance with the stage manager.

‘Let's give him a try,’ he said finally, and shoved Jarli past the curtain onto the stage.

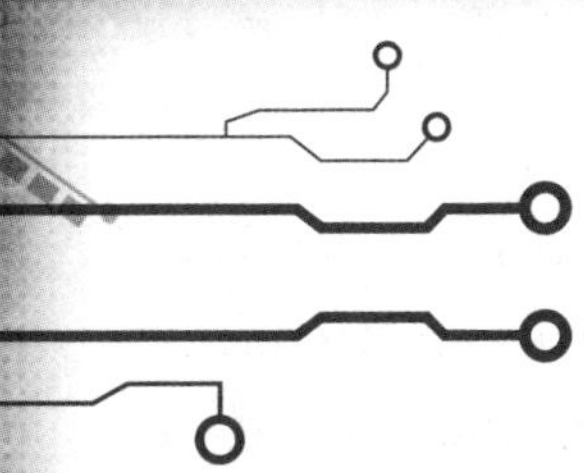

HAMMER TIME

'Please welcome our first competitor,' Plowman announced, 'Jarli Durras, creator of Sir Ramington!'

There was a polite smattering of applause. Someone yelled, 'Woo!' It sounded like Bess.

Jarli suddenly found himself facing the crowd. Not every seat was full—this was Kelton, after all—but at least two hundred people were here, staring at him. Many of them he knew. His whole science class from school was here, although the stage lights were too bright to make out most of the faces. He could see the teacher, Mrs Prive, and the school nurse, Maria Eaton.

Jarli wondered why the nurse was here. Maybe it was dangerous, taking a ringside seat to a robot fight. Jarli had never attended one before. Would sharp pieces of metal be flying out of the ring?

He shot Eaton a nervous smile. She didn't smile back, which was typical. She was a former army surgeon, perpetually serious.

Jarli looked for Bess, but couldn't see her through

the glare. Hopefully she had a good seat.

Jarli had wanted his mum and dad to come, but they couldn't. Six months ago, Cobra—an assassin working for Viper—had rammed Dad's car. Jarli and Dad had survived the crash, but some scars on Dad's face still weren't healing properly. Right now Mum was taking him to a follow-up appointment with Dr Vorham, a skin specialist who had once treated Jarli for nitrogen burns. By the time Jarli got home, Dad would probably be asleep and Mum would be at her second job.

It wasn't just the scars. Privately, Jarli worried about Dad's brain, too. His head had been banged around in the crash, and lately he'd been forgetful. He walked around the house like he wasn't sure where things were kept. Old friends would phone, and he didn't seem to know who they were right away. Sometimes Mum had to call his name several times before he responded.

Jarli was about to turn away from the crowd when he noticed a man and a woman in dark business suits. They were whispering to each other. The woman was in her twenties, with thick eyebrows and a flat nose. The other guy was older, with a square face and a little moustache. His dark eyes were focused on Jarli.

Jarli's skin crawled. He hated being the centre of

attention. He didn't even post selfies. When his app went viral and he had briefly become a celebrity, it had been a nightmare. And these two people didn't look like parents or robotics nerds. Why were they staring at him like that?

Turning his back on them, he squinted against the blinding stage lights. The arena was a square platform surrounded by tough transparent plastic, like a small hockey rink. Sir Ramington was already in one corner. He was basically a battering ram on wheels, with pincers at one end. In the opposite corner was a much larger robot, bright pink and shaped like a giant hammer with tank treads on either side. Chloe.

'And a roboticist from interstate,' Plowman continued, his voice booming through the PA system. 'Rebecca Lieu, creator of Chloe!'

The girl with the Harry Potter glasses emerged from behind the curtain to stand next to Jarli. Jarli forced a friendly smile at her. She didn't return it.

Plowman stood at a lectern on the far side of the stage. 'There will be three rounds,' Plowman said. 'Each robot will attempt to push the other onto the trapdoor in the corner . . .'

'How'd you pick that name?' Rebecca whispered to Jarli.

'What?'

'The name. Sir Ramington. How'd you pick it?'

'I didn't,' Jarli said. 'My teammate did.'

Rebecca crossed her arms over her chest. 'Well, it's almost identical to the name of my friend's robot.'

Jarli said nothing.

'And the robot itself is very similar,' Rebecca added.

'Your friend must have good taste in robots.'

'Had,' Rebecca said. 'He's dead.'

Jarli's eyes widened. Doug's old friends thought he was *dead?*

'I'm sorry,' he said.

'It's not OK to steal a design off a dead person,' Rebecca said. 'How did you even find out about it?'

'I didn't steal anything,' Jarli said, and waited for her app to verify that he was telling the truth.

But she just glared at him.

'I'm not lying,' Jarli added. 'Check your app.'

'All phones are off,' Rebecca said. 'Didn't you hear the announcements?'

Jarli sighed. The one time he actually wanted someone to be using his app, and they weren't.

Rebecca pulled a wireless video-game controller out of her satchel. 'You're going down,' she told Jarli. Then she frowned. 'Hey. Where's *your* controller?'

'Human reflexes are too slow,' Jarli said. 'Sir Ramington is autonomous.'

Rebecca snorted. 'Good luck with that.'

Plowman had finished outlining the rules. 'Round one,' he said, 'starts . . . now!'

There was a loud *beep,* and a red light turned green. Jarli held his breath as Chloe zoomed across the arena. Sir Ramington was great at chasing targets, but not so good at dodging obstacles, particularly moving ones. And Chloe was moving *fast.*

Sir Ramington remained perfectly still as Chloe approached. Soon he was in range of her fearsome hammer.

A latch clicked and a spring rattled as Chloe unfolded, swinging the hammer up, over and down—

But Jarli's program kicked in and Sir Ramington darted sideways, just in time. The hammer hit the floor behind him with a loud *WHACK.*

Someone in the crowd cheered.

Unfortunately, Sir Ramington had gone the wrong way. Wheels whirring, he zoomed right onto a trapdoor. It fell open and Sir Ramington plunged straight through.

The cheers from the audience turned to laughter. Jarli put his face in his hands.

'Nice AI,' Rebecca commented. 'I've never seen robot with a death-wish before.'

The scoreboard flashed:

	TOTAL	RD1	RD2	RD3
SIR RAMINGTON V	0	0	0	0
CHLOE	1	1	0	0

A stagehand retrieved Sir Ramington from the net under the arena and plonked him back on the stage.

'Round two,' Plowman said. If Rebecca won this round as well, Jarli and Doug would be eliminated from the competition.

There was another *beep,* and another green light.

Chewing her lip, Rebecca drove Chloe straight towards Sir Ramington again. This had worked last time, so she probably assumed it would work again. But she had underestimated Jarli's code. He had programmed Sir Ramington to learn from his failures.

This time Sir Ramington rolled the other way when Chloe approached. Again, the fearsome hammer missed. Ramington swivelled to face Chloe and latched onto the pink robot's side with his pincers. Chloe was facing the wrong way to use the hammer. She tried to turn, but Ramington just turned with it. Chloe couldn't shake him off.

'Come on,' Jarli whispered. 'Do it!'

Now Sir Ramington did what he was best at. Keeping a firm grip, he pushed his mighty wheels forward and rammed the other bot against the tough plastic wall.

'Woo!' yelled someone in the crowd. Probably Bess again.

But Chloe was a tough robot. She looked unharmed.

Sir Ramington rammed the wall again. Still no damage to the other robot. Rebecca was fiddling furiously with the remote, trying to get back in control.

Too late. Ramington dragged Chloe over to the trapdoor. It fell open, and Chloe plummeted through—

But Ramington's pincers didn't release her in time. Ramington fell through the trapdoor as well.

More laughter from the audience. The scoreboard flickered, but the score remained unchanged. Apparently they had both lost, rather than both winning.

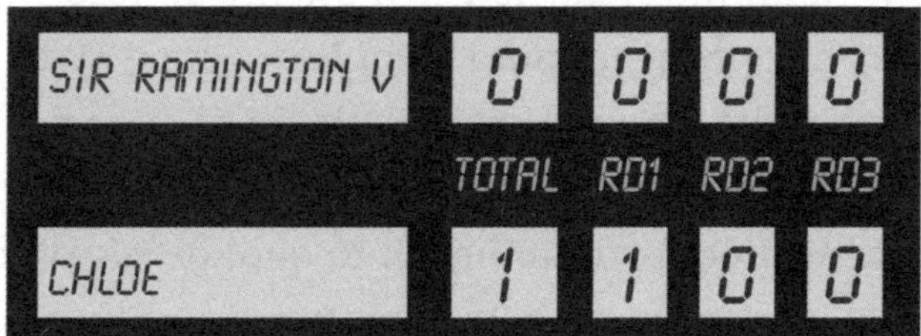

'No score draw,' Plowman announced. 'If Sir Ramington wins round three, there will be a tie breaker.'

Rebecca gritted her teeth as both robots were returned to the arena. Jarli jammed his hands in his pockets, hoping the audience couldn't tell how anxious he was.

Beep! The light turned green.

Chloe launched forward. This time, Sir Ramington didn't even try to avoid her. He accelerated towards the bigger robot. Ramming speed.

'No, no, no!' Jarli muttered under his breath. 'What are you *doing?*' Soon Ramington would be within the hammer's range.

Too late. Rebecca pushed a button, and the hammer came down.

It hit Sir Ramington with a huge crash. One of his wheels went flying. Another got jammed, and wouldn't turn.

Jarli cringed. The crowd gasped.

'Got you!' Rebecca said.

Sir Ramington turned around in agitated little circles, his programming unable to cope with the damage to the wheels. Jarli watched as Chloe pushed him slowly across the arena towards the trapdoor.

Jarli waited for Ramington to engage his pincers and pull Chloe down with him, but the robot didn't do it. The trapdoor opened, and Sir Ramington fell out of sight, alone.

Jarli felt a pang of disappointment.

Rebecca turned to face the crowd, eyes shining—

And all the colour drained from her face.

Jarli turned to see what she was looking at, and saw Doug trying to sneak out the front door. The side entrance must have been locked—or maybe he hadn't been able to resist watching the battle.

Rebecca stared at Doug, her dead friend, for another second. Then she screamed.

BACK FROM THE DEAD

For a moment, nobody moved.

Doug froze on his way out the door. Some people in the crowd turned to look at him, while others kept staring in alarm at Rebecca, who was still screaming. Jarli hovered next to her, not sure what to do.

When Rebecca ran out of air and fell silent, everyone else started talking at once.

'Are you OK, Miss?'

'What's wrong with her?'

'Everybody stay calm—'

'She saw something in the crowd, like maybe a gun, or a—'

'Gun? Who's got a gun?!'

Doug's paralysis broke and he ran out the door. This made everyone else even more alarmed. People scrambled out of their seats and ran for the exits, looking over their shoulders and bumping into each other. The kids from Jarli's science class babbled as Mrs Prive tried to reassure them. Maria Eaton jostled past, making her way to the stage.

Jarli was the only one who understood what was happening. He touched Rebecca's arm. 'Listen to me,' he said. 'It's not what you think.'

Rebecca didn't seem to hear him. She trembled as she stared at the door where Doug had been a second ago.

Plowman stormed across the stage towards them. 'What's going on?' he demanded. 'Is this some kind of prank?'

Maria Eaton, the school nurse, had reached the stage. 'I have medical training,' she told Plowman and Rebecca. 'Can I help?'

While Jarli was frantically trying to work out what to say, Rebecca fled. She sprinted off the stage before anyone could stop her.

'Wait!' Jarli gave chase. If Rebecca started telling everyone about her dead friend's ghost, people would use Jarli's app to check her story. They would realise that Rebecca believed she was telling the truth. Someone would figure out the real story, and soon Doug's secret identity would be exposed. Jarli already felt guilty about the danger his app had put Doug in. He couldn't let the damage get any worse.

Jarli found Rebecca backstage. The stage manager had grabbed Rebecca's arm, but it looked like she had no clue what else to do.

'Don't touch me!' Rebecca shook off the stage

manager's hand. The woman backed off.

'Rebecca!' Jarli hissed. 'That wasn't a ghost, OK?'

She looked at him. Her terror was contagious. Jarli felt equally frightened, even though he knew what was going on. No wonder everyone else had panicked and ran outside.

Jarli took a deep breath. He didn't want to betray Doug's trust. But if he didn't, soon everyone would discover the secret.

'Terence isn't dead,' he whispered. 'He's been living here under another name. OK?'

'He's what?'

'He's in hiding.' Jarli pulled out his phone and switched it on so he could prove that he was telling the truth. 'But you can't tell anyone.'

'What do you mean?' The confusion on Rebecca's face was morphing into anger.

Jarli was about to explain, when he saw the suits—the mysterious man and woman who had been staring at him from the audience. They had followed him, and now they were trying to talk their way past the stage manager.

Jarli thought of the strange feeling he'd had in the queue outside. The sense of being watched.

Those two are after me. They must work for Viper!

Doug wasn't the only one with a target on his back. Viper had also tried to kill Jarli just a few months ago. Maybe he had decided to try again, knowing that Doug and Jarli would both be at the battle.

'I've gotta go,' Jarli hissed.

He abandoned the furious Rebecca and ran towards the side exit, the door leading to the alley. But when he grabbed the handle, it wouldn't turn. He'd forgotten it had locked itself behind him after the stage manager had let them in. Jarli was trapped!

Heart pounding, he quickly scanned the backstage area. The bathroom was useless. They would find him. But there was a fire door nearby, with a sign: THIS DOOR IS ALARMED. Fire doors were never locked. There was some kind of law.

He sprinted towards the door, weaving through the confused competitors.

'There he is!' the woman in the suit shouted.

Jarli pushed down on the crash bar and burst into the daylight. An alarm started clanging like a jackhammer above his head. A siren wailed through the building.

He found himself in a narrow alley between the town hall and the cinema. He looked left and saw cars and people, a busy street by Kelton standards. He looked right and saw a dead end. Jarli turned left, sprinting towards the busy road, hoping to disappear amongst the other pedestrians.

As he ran, he heard someone crash through the fire door behind him. Leather shoes slapped the concrete. More than one set—both the suits must be chasing him. And it sounded like they were catching up.

I have to get out of sight, now!

Jarli reached the end of the alley and made a sharp right turn towards the cinema, startling two old men. He was out of sight. Now he needed to disappear.

There was another alley on the opposite side of the street, between Kelton Public Library and the ugliest building in the whole town, a windowless concrete slab signposted **THE J.R. LIST CENTRE.** The alley looked like a good hiding place. Jarli ran onto the road.

Tyres screeched as something hurtled out of Jarli's peripheral vision. A car, the same shade of grey as the asphalt.

If Jarli had stayed still, the impact would have broken both his legs. Instead he threw himself sideways, covering his face with his hands. The car banged against his shins when he was in midair. He rolled sideways across the bonnet and hit the road with a thud.

No time to recover. He scrambled to his feet and hobbled dizzily towards the alley—

A big hand grabbed his collar. Jarli jerked backwards like he'd hit a wall.

'Take it easy, mate,' the square-faced man in the suit said. 'We just want to talk to you.'

The window of the car rolled down. The driver was a wide-eyed man with receding hair and a checked shirt.

'What the heck were you thinking?' he yelled at Jarli.

The woman in the suit spoke to the driver. 'Don't worry, we got him. We'll make sure he's alright.'

'Be more careful,' the driver snapped, and rolled the window back up. The car cruised away.

Jarli looked up at the two people in suits, heart pounding. They sure did have him, but what for?

The square-faced man released Jarli's collar.

'Jarli Durras,' the heavy-browed woman said. 'Right?'

'No,' Jarli said, unconvincingly.

LIE The man's and the woman's phones both beeped. So did Jarli's.

The man smirked. The woman looked annoyed.

'Are you hurt?' she asked.

Jarli looked down. His palms hurt from scraping the asphalt, but they weren't bleeding. His ankles throbbed, but they held him up.

'I don't think so,' Jarli said. 'Who are you?'

'My name's Norma Sellick,' the woman said. She looked at Jarli as though he was supposed to recognise the name. He didn't.

'I'm the Assistant Minister for Defence,' Sellick added. 'This is Agent Lindsay.'

'What do you want?'

'Just a few minutes of your time,' Sellick said. 'Come with us.'

A crowd grew in front of the town hall. After emerging from the front door, most people just stopped on the steps, trapping more and more anxious spectators behind them. No-one wanted to be inside, but everyone was too curious to go home.

Everyone except Doug. He was already ahead of the crowd, darting between the pedestrians out on the street.

His dad wouldn't be here to pick him up until five, when the Robattle had been scheduled to finish. Doug couldn't wait that long. He had to escape before—

'Terence!' someone shrieked.

Doug recognised Rebecca's voice. He'd never heard her so angry. He just ran, not thinking anything except, *Get away, get away!*

He shoved people aside as he ran away from the town hall. 'Sorry, sorry,' he muttered.

'Hey!' someone yelled as he pushed past.

Doug turned a corner and bolted, heading for the library. The smell of scorched rubber hung in the air, along with a haze of blue smoke. Fresh tyre marks lined the asphalt. Something just happened here. No time to think about it.

He was almost at the library. It was oddly shaped, like a jigsaw piece, with lots of hiding places outside and in. Rebecca didn't know this town. She wouldn't find him there. If he hid for long enough, she might wonder if he had been somebody else. She couldn't have seen his face clearly.

The thought of tricking his old friend into thinking she hadn't seen him made Doug feel horrible. But it was better than being exposed, and having his whole family murdered by Viper.

Something slammed into his back, and he tripped. Rebecca had thrown her handbag at him.

'Ow!' he complained.

'You let me think you were *dead!*' Rebecca snarled.

Dead? Doug cringed. He had thought Rebecca would assume he'd moved away without saying goodbye. He hadn't realised that she would think he was dead. A horrible feeling twisted his guts.

He rolled over. 'I didn't—'

'Do you have any idea what I've been through?' Tears streamed down Rebecca's cheeks.

It was hard to look at her. When Doug first moved to Kelton, he had spent every waking moment wondering what she was doing. He had been furious at his parents for dragging him to this middle-of-nowhere town. But over time he had thought about her less and less. Seeing her in person brought everything back, with an extra helping of guilt.

'My life was in danger,' he said.

'*Now* your life's in danger,' Rebecca snapped, snatching up her handbag and throwing it at him again.

'Stop hitting me!' Doug tried to crawl away, but Rebecca crouched next to him on the footpath and grabbed the front of his shirt.

'The teachers said you were sick,' she said, her voice wobbling. 'I went to your house to check on you, and you weren't there. I went to the hospital, and they wouldn't tell me if you were there or not. When you didn't come back after a week, I knew you must be really sick—and then I heard one of the year-eight kids saying you were dead. Suddenly lots of people were saying that, and—'

'Why would you believe some year-eight kid?' Doug demanded.

'Because you never called! You never messaged me—not even a single emoji. A thumbs-up would have done. I thought if you were alive, there was no way you'd leave me wondering what had happened to you for an *entire year.*'

People were staring at them through the windows of the library, eyes wide. Doug felt his face go red.

'The police took my phone,' he hissed. 'They told me if I tried to get in touch with anyone, my family would be in danger. I couldn't contact you.'

'As if! You could have emailed me. You could have borrowed someone's phone. All you had to do was tell me what was going on, and I would have kept it a secret. But you didn't trust me. It was easier to let me think you got hit by a bus, or got some deadly disease, or—'

'You think this year has been easy for me? You have no idea what I've been through.'

'You're right.' Rebecca gripped his shirt even tighter. 'I don't. That's the whole problem. At least you knew where I was. I knew nothing. You were my best friend, Terence.'

It felt strange, hearing his old name out loud. He had been Doug for so long that he didn't feel like Terence anymore. 'You were my *only* friend,' he said. 'And you hardly saw me even before I left. You were always busy with your new mates.'

Rebecca let go of him, stung. 'You ungrateful—'

'Ungrateful? Because I wasn't cool enough to be your real friend anymore, right? But you sometimes hung out with me anyway. Out of pity.'

Rebecca looked like she was trying to talk, but she was too angry even to form the words. Then she turned, and walked away.

'You're not going to tell anyone,' Doug called, suddenly nervous. 'Right?'

Rebecca didn't even look back. Soon she was gone.

Doug rested the back of his head against the cool concrete and looked up at the cloudless blue sky.

He went through the conversation, counting all the things he wished he hadn't said: six. He'd stuffed that up, badly.

As Doug sat up, he saw someone watching him from the other side of the street. A figure crouched in the branches of a tree, semi-hidden in the shadows. Doug couldn't see a face, because it was concealed by a BLOOD-RED SCARF.

Like everyone else, Doug had heard the rumours of the masked figure roaming Kelton by night. But he hadn't really believed them. He certainly hadn't expected to see the figure in broad daylight.

'Hey,' he called, climbing to his feet.

The masked figure—a teen girl, maybe?—

dropped to the ground as silently as a cat.

Doug started to walk towards her, but she ran in the opposite direction. Doug gave chase. But he was still puffed from his last run, and the masked figure was incredibly fast. As Doug's feet pounded the asphalt, he watched the girl disappear around the corner behind an old car wash in seconds. By the time Doug got to the corner, she was out of sight.

He turned around and around, confused and worried. Nothing but empty streets. Who was she? Had she heard all of his conversation with Rebecca?

And now that she knew his secret, what would she do with it?

TABLE FOR SMITH

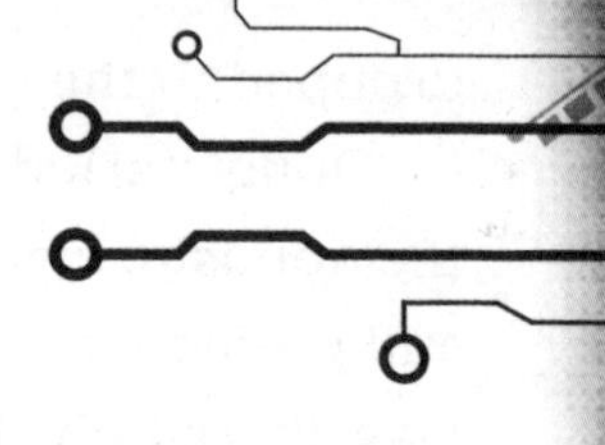

The two suits took Jarli to the café next to the cinema. The peeling sign above the door said simply, KELTON COFFEEHOUSE.

As they walked in, the waitress hurried over—a girl named Nadia from Jarli's school. Her parents owned the café, and she was friends with Jarli's sister, so she had been to his house a couple of times.

'Hey Jarls,' she said. 'Who are your friends?'

'Table for Smith,' Sellick said as they walked in. Jarli couldn't remember the man's name—agent something-or-other—but he was pretty sure it wasn't Smith.

'Smith? You're early,' Nadia said. 'You booked for five-fifteen.'

Jarli's captors looked around at the empty café.

'So what?' asked the agent.

Jarli blinked furiously at Nadia, trying to signal to her that these guys were trouble. But she had already turned away.

'Come on, then,' she said.

She led them over to a table in the back corner, away from the windows. No-one outside would see them or come to Jarli's aid.

Nadia dumped some menus on the table and slipped away.

'What do you want?' Jarli asked again.

'I'm the head of ministerial security,' the agent said. He showed Jarli a badge, and an ID card which gave his full name: **WILLIAM LINDSAY.**

Jarli's phone didn't beep. Lindsay was telling the truth. But a government job wasn't proof that he didn't also work for Viper. A Kelton police officer—Constable Blanco—was still suspended pending an investigation about her connections to the criminal mastermind.

'Uh-huh,' Jarli said.

Sellick spoke without looking up from the menu. 'We're here ahead of the conference.'

'What conference?' Jarli asked.

Sellick and Lindsay looked at each other.

'Don't get smart with us, kid,' Lindsay said.

'I'm not smart. I mean, I am—but I don't know what you're talking about.'

'That'd be right,' Lindsay said to Sellick. 'A tiny little town like this gets to host a major tech summit, and the locals don't even know about it.'

Jarli bristled. 'Just because you've never heard

of Kelton before,' he said, 'doesn't mean nothing happens here.'

Sellick held up her hands. 'OK. On Friday there's a conference at Kellin Plowman's golf resort. Heads of hardware and software companies will meet with representatives from the Defence Department. Basically, people who make robots will mingle with people who buy robots. With us so far?'

Jarli was confused. 'Has this got something to do with the Robattle?'

'The Robattle is a small part of a much larger event. The main conference isn't open to the public.'

'Oh. Right.' Now Jarli was starting to remember. Bess's mum ran the only taxi company in town, and she'd said something about the conference. She was looking forward to the extra business.

Jarli's phone dinged. A message from Bess.

You sure know how to make an exit. Want to tell me what just happened?

'Turn that off,' Lindsay said sharply. 'This is a confidential discussion.'

Reluctantly, Jarli did. From now on, anything they said could be untrue, and he wouldn't know.

Nadia was back. 'Are you ready to order?'

'Thank you,' Sellick said. 'I'll have a mineral water.'

'Coffee,' Lindsay said. 'Long black.' He looked at Jarli. 'We're buying. You want . . . I dunno, a babycino?'

Nadia smirked.

Jarli felt his face grow hot. He glared at Lindsay. 'How old do you think I am?'

Lindsay shrugged. 'I guess that'll be all,' he said, handing the menus back to Nadia.

With an exaggerated sigh, Nadia slouched off to the kitchen.

'The Minister for Defence is hoping you'll be there,' Sellick said to Jarli.

'Where?'

'At the conference.'

Jarli's eyes bugged out. 'Why?'

She smiled. 'To demonstrate this government's commitment to transparency.'

'What does that mean?'

'It means that we want you to use the *Truth* app on Mr Fisher—the Minister for Defence—while he makes his speech,' Lindsay said.

'In case he lies?' Jarli was puzzled. Why would they want to catch out their own boss?

'To prove that he's telling the truth,' Lindsay said, like it was obvious. 'Mr Fisher wants—'

He fell silent as Nadia came back with the drinks. Nadia seemed to have finally noticed the weird, secretive manner of the two government operatives. She looked curiously at Jarli before she walked away. She would probably start messaging his sister as soon as she was out of sight.

'Unfortunately,' Sellick said, 'the public's trust in the government has reached an all-time low.'

'Thanks to you,' Lindsay added. 'Your app has got three ministers fired.'

'Not my fault,' Jarli said. 'They shouldn't have lied.'

'It's not as simple as that. Sometimes you have to lie to protect someone else. Or—'

Sellick silenced him with a sharp look. 'It's not just a government problem,' she said, changing the topic slightly. 'Companies are asking workers questions like, 'Were you honestly unwell when you took a sick day two years ago?' Customers are asking salespeople, 'Is this item cheaper at any other stores?' People are losing their jobs all over the place, and they can't get new ones because they can't lie in the job interviews. The courts are struggling to work out if it's legal to fire someone because of an app. Meanwhile, convicted criminals are demanding retrials, claiming that your app proves their innocence. The nation is in chaos, and it's only getting worse. Did you know your app is banned in three countries?'

'Smart move, in my view,' Lindsay said.

Jarli had heard about this. Technically it was *Truth Premium,* the much more successful rip-off of his app, which had been banned. But Jarli didn't say anything.

Sellick sipped her sparkling water. 'Trust will be key at this conference. The parties have to trust each other for the negotiations, and the public must not be suspicious about the deals being made behind closed doors. That's why we want you there.'

Jarli frowned. 'Anybody can use my app,' he said. 'You don't need any special skills. You don't even have to be there in person. Anyone could use it on a high-definition video of Fisher's speech if they wanted to be sure he was telling the truth.'

'We're painfully aware of that,' Lindsay said. 'It's not just about the app. Having Truth Boy there—'

'Truth Boy?' Jarli cringed. Did people really call him that? It sounded like the world's lamest superhero.

'—is a symbol of this government's honesty.'

'Right,' Jarli said slowly. It sounded like his worst nightmare. He hated being the centre of attention.

'We already booked you a room at Plowman's resort for tomorrow,' Sellick said.

Jarli had never been inside the huge luxury hotel on the edge of town. The car park was nearly always empty, since Kelton had few visitors and the motel was much cheaper. Kellin Plowman had built the resort just because he had money to burn and he liked golf.

There were so many things wrong with all this that Jarli didn't know where to begin. 'You know I live here, right?' he said. 'You don't have to get me a hotel room. And what about school?'

'We need you on-site,' Sellick said. 'Makes it easier for Agent Lindsay and the rest of the security personnel to keep an eye on you. Don't worry about school. We've already arranged things with your principal.'

'I haven't even said yes yet.'

'What's the problem?' Lindsay said. 'I thought a country kid like you would jump at the chance for some excitement.'

Jarli gritted his teeth. He had experienced more than enough excitement. In just the last six months, he had been in a car wreck, trapped in a warehouse fire and witnessed a plane crash. He had been shot at, lied to and burned with liquid nitrogen, all thanks to Viper.

He opened his mouth to tell the suits to get lost.

'How is your father, Jarli?' Sellick said suddenly. 'I'm sorry, I should have asked earlier.'

'My father?'

'Yeah,' Lindsay said. 'We heard he's still in hospital after a car accident.'

'You heard wrong,' Jarli said. 'He was discharged pretty soon after. He's just visiting the hospital for check-ups.'

'But he's had a few of those check-ups, right? Seems like he's in and out of there all the time. How is he holding down a job?'

'He's stopped working for a bit,' Jarli said uncertainly. 'So Mum's working more instead.'

'Is she?' Sellick looked surprised. 'That must be hard on her.'

'It's nice that your parents don't burden you and your sister with their money troubles,' Lindsay said.

'Anyway,' Sellick said. 'Glad your dad's OK. Did we mention that you'd be compensated for your presence at the conference?'

'Generously compensated,' Lindsay added. 'Plus, you'll get a lot of media exposure. If you're smart about this, you could turn that into a lot of money. Our public relations people might be able to help with that.'

Sellick finished her drink without taking her eyes of Jarli.

Jarli wasn't a fool. He could tell that they were manipulating him. But he wondered if they were right. Dad had been at the hospital a lot since the crash, and Mum always seemed tired and worried. How much money did they have? She certainly hadn't wanted to help Jarli buy the new *Snake Man* game.

'How much money are we talking?' Jarli asked hesitantly.

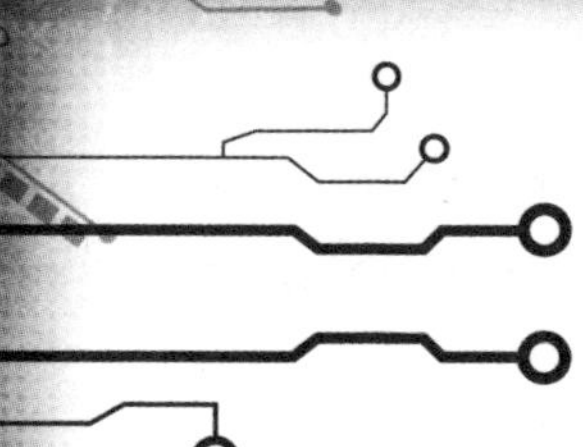

PENALTY FOR DISOBEDIENCE

Horsham's phone rang, and he dropped his laptop. It hit the concrete, corner first. The battery came loose, and the power light turned an ominous orange before it died.

Horsham swore. He wasn't usually clumsy. But he was still getting used to his new arms. The bones had been broken, reset and reinforced with CARBON-FIBRE RODS. They were stronger now, but the extra length made them harder to manipulate.

The phone was still buzzing in his desk drawer. It had to be Viper. No-one else ever called that phone.

'Hey, new guy. You OK?' Niyoko asked. She was the other guard on duty—a dark-haired woman with cat's eye glasses and a small stature, who nevertheless terrified the prisoners.

'Yeah, fine,' Horsham mumbled. 'Just dropped my laptop.'

'I see that,' Niyoko said drily. 'You look like this place is getting to you.'

'I'm fine,' Horsham said again. He stooped to

pick up the pieces of his laptop. Hopefully he could fix it himself. He couldn't take it to a repair shop. There were things on it no-one else was allowed to see.

The phone had been ringing for fifteen seconds now. Soon Viper would give up. And then what?

'Let me get that for you.' Niyoko opened the desk drawer and lifted up the phone.

'No!' Horsham snatched the phone out of Niyoko's hand and answered it.

'This is Horsham,' he said. 'But it's not a great time.'

Viper's voice was distorted, as always. An alien growl: 'Make it a good time.'

Niyoko was helpfully jamming the battery into the laptop. She gave him a thumbs-up. 'It's cool, I got this.'

Horsham couldn't tell her to stop without making her suspicious. But the hard drive was encrypted. Hopefully she wouldn't notice anything out of the ordinary while she was tinkering.

He stepped out the door of the office, into the narrow corridors of Throwaway. The inmates called it that—as in, *Throw away the key*. The concrete walls were two metres thick,with no windows. The silence sometimes left Horsham's ears ringing, as though he'd been deafened by an artillery shell. From in here, there was no sign that the rest of the world existed. It was like working on a space station.

A space station full of spies, criminals and lunatics.

He walked into the break room and closed the door, putting some extra distance between himself and Niyoko. The coffee machine dripped a growing stain onto a benchtop. Rats were skitter-scattering behind the fridge. *No prison is so secret that rats won't find it,* Horsham thought.

There was a grimy mirror above the sink. Horsham caught a glimpse of his face—his new face—and looked away. It was impossible to get used to.

He took a deep breath, and put the phone to his ear. 'OK,' he said.

Horsham had never met Viper. It seemed like no-one had. But he had seen a blurry photograph once, of a man with horrible burns around his mouth, his eyes hidden behind the brim of a black hat.

'I have another task for you,' Viper said. 'Do I need to remind you of the penalty for disobedience?'

'No.' Horsham scratched the scar on the back of his hand. He could feel the RFID chip underneath, ready to release a dose of poison if Viper pushed the button.

The poison, he knew, was snake venom. Viper

had a sick sense of humour.

'Excellent,' Viper said. 'It's time to take your new face out for a spin. Agent Lindsay will be removed within hours. You're going to take his place. There's a red sedan parked near the public library. Registration SNK-817. The keys are under the wheel well. Inside you'll find equipment, and detailed instructions.'

'What's my mission?' Horsham asked.

Even through the distortion, he could hear the smile in Viper's voice. 'You're going to kill the Minister for Defence.'

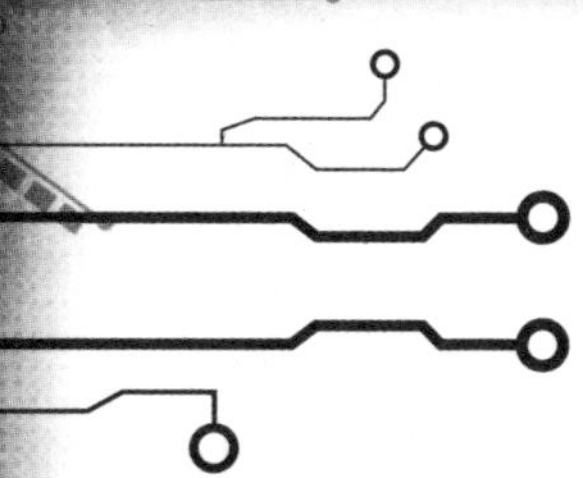

SENT TO HIS DOOM

Jarli stared gloomily at the clothes on his bed. A shirt, a light jacket and some new-ish jeans which weren't frayed yet. Sellick had told him to pack his nicest clothes. This outfit wasn't exactly a three-piece suit, but it would have to do.

He put on the jacket and stuffed the other clothes into his schoolbag—he didn't own a suitcase—and walked into the bathroom to grab his toothbrush. It was ridiculous, packing for a trip to a golf resort that was only just out of town. This whole situation felt like something out of a dream. Not a nightmare, exactly. Just one of those confusing dreams where things make no sense, but no-one else seems to notice.

Mum appeared in the bathroom doorway. Her hair was all frizzy and she had bags under her eyes from the night shift at the supermarket.

'How's Dad?' Jarli asked.

'Asleep. I don't want to wake him. He got back from the hospital very late last night, and Doctor Vorham says he needs plenty of rest.'

Mum sighed. 'Feels like we've hardly seen him lately.'

Jarli didn't like the sound of that. A month after the car crash, Dad had seemed fine. Now he spent all his time either at the hospital or sleeping at home in the spare room. If Doctor Vorham was so great, why was Dad getting worse?

'When will you be back?' Mum asked.

'I'm not even really going anywhere,' Jarli said, exasperated. 'They only need me for the first day of the conference, which is tomorrow. So I'll be back tomorrow night, I think.'

'You think?'

Jarli shrugged. As soon as he had agreed to Sellick's deal, she and Lindsay had stopped giving him information.

His phone dinged. He checked it. A message from Doug.

So, Rebecca's still angry. But I don't think she's going to tell anyone.

'You know you don't have to do this, right?' Mum asked.

Jarli dropped some toothpaste and a hairbrush into a waterproof bag. 'I don't?'

'Of course not.' Mum squeezed his shoulder.

'They're not the boss of you. You don't have to present at a conference just because someone asked you to.'

'I'm not exactly presenting,' Jarli grumbled. He walked back to the bedroom and shoved his bathroom bag into the backpack.

Mum followed him in. 'What's going on, sweetheart?'

'Nothing,' Jarli said.

Mum's phone beeped. LIE She raised an eyebrow.

Jarli sighed. 'Don't worry, OK?' he said. 'Surely you've got enough to think about. With . . . you know.'

'With what?'

'With Dad.'

'Your father will be fine. You don't need to worry.'

The phone didn't beep. But just because Mum wasn't lying, that didn't mean she was right. If Dad was fine, why did he need to keep visiting the hospital? And what if Mum lost one of her jobs, or they ran out of money before he was better?

Kirstie burst into the bathroom. 'Mum! The wi-fi's stopped working.'

'Shh!' Mum said. 'Your father's sleeping.'

'I'll fix it,' Jarli said absently.

'Hurry! I'm in the middle of a video chat. I don't

want to use up all my data.' Kirstie vanished again.

Jarli was about to leave the bedroom when Mum swept him into a hug. 'You're a good kid,' she said. 'But you have to remember, not everything is your problem. You can't carry the whole world around on your shoulders. You'll get squashed.'

I'm not trying to carry the world, he thought. *Just you and Dad.*

'OK,' he said, half expecting the app to beep again. It didn't, and he wondered what that meant.

Jarli carried his bag out to the lounge room, where he was surprised to see Dad was awake and on the couch. The TV was on, but the sound was off. Dad didn't seem to be watching it. Jarli got the feeling he had been listening to the conversation with Mum in the bathroom.

'Everything OK, sport?' he said.

Dad never called Jarli 'sport'. It was like he was putting on false cheer. Pretending everything was normal.

Jarli didn't want to stress Dad out. 'Don't worry about me.'

'It's my job,' Dad said.

Jarli changed the subject. 'You want me to put the kettle on?'

Dad rubbed his eyes and winced. 'Sure, if you're having something. I'll have a coffee.'

'You're sure?' Jarli asked. Dad was usually a tea drinker—he'd always told Jarli that coffee was 'as bitter as the fifth Beatle'.

'Yup. I could use the caffeine.'

Jarli flicked on the kettle and spooned some instant coffee into a mug. There was no wall between the kitchen and the lounge room, so he could watch Dad's reflection in the glass of the microwave. Dad just sat there like a zombie. Jarli's heart ached.

The kettle boiled just as the doorbell rang.

'That'll be the government,' Jarli said gloomily. He poured the boiling water into Dad's cup and then walked towards the front door.

'Don't trust them,' Dad said.

Jarli froze in the hallway. He was about to ask what Dad meant when Mum entered the lounge room.

'You're up,' Mum said, patting Dad's head.

Dad grunted as he got up to retrieve his coffee. 'The G-men are here to pick up Jarli.'

'I heard the bell.' Mum ran over and gave Jarli another hug. 'Good luck, sweetheart. And don't worry about us. OK?'

Jarli picked up his bag again. A shirt, some jeans and a toothbrush had never felt so heavy.

The car was a luxurious sedan with leather seats and unnecessarily powerful air conditioning. It was like entering a walk-in freezer. Jarli rubbed his forearms as he sat down.

A woman he'd never met before was in the driver's seat. She wore a business suit, a gold watch and leather gloves. She looked with hollow eyes at Jarli in the rear-view mirror.

'It's a fifteen-minute drive,' she said. 'You packed good clothes?'

'Yes,' Jarli said. He didn't add that they were almost the same as the clothes he was wearing.

'Great.' The woman programmed an address into her phone navigation—she must not be local—and then put her foot down. The car zoomed off towards the hotel. 'You don't have to say anything. Just stand there with your phone up while Fisher is talking.'

'Who's Fisher, again?'

The woman sighed. 'The Minister for Defence.'

Oh. Jarli hadn't been concentrating. Since the crash, he found it hard to make conversation in a car. He was always watching the road, waiting for a vehicle to zoom out of the shadows and smash into him. He would scan the faces of the other drivers to see if any of them was COBRA—the old man who had rammed Dad's car. An assassin, working for Viper, who still haunted Jarli's nightmares.

'There will be no questions from the journalists,' the woman continued. 'If they ask any, ignore them. Agent Lindsay is the head of the minister's personal security. You met him?'

Jarli nodded wordlessly.

'Great. He'll greet you in the lobby. Just do everything he says.'

The conversation dried up. Jarli used the opportunity to respond to Doug's text.

Glad she won't tell anyone. But why is she angry? You didn't do anything wrong.

Doug's response was immediate.

Yeah, that's what I said. Didn't help.

There's something else I have to tell you.

What?

I saw the Red Ninja. I think it's a teenager.

Jarli stared at the screen uneasily. It was one thing for strangers to talk about seeing the masked figure. But if Doug had seen it, the rumours were true.

Where? What happened?

'We're here,' the driver said.

Jarli looked up from his phone. He had never seen the Kelton Golf Resort up close—it wasn't on the way to anywhere. But it always loomed on the horizon. Two curved buildings, surrounded by imported palm trees. The hills around it were blanketed by perfect grass. *It's too neat,* thought Jarli. *It doesn't look real.*

The hotel was busy, staff scurrying around making preparations for the delegates and the media. Guards chattered on walkie-talkies, sweating in formal suits. Window washers dangled from the roof, polishing the glass on the fifth floor. People in black polo shirts were unfolding tripods near the hotel entrance. They worked for the news crews, Jarli supposed.

The woman stopped the car. Jarli climbed out, squinting in the sun. He hadn't brought a hat.

The car zoomed away towards the car park, leaving him standing alone in the driveway.

'Jarli Durras!'

Jarli turned around. His heart sank when he recognised the piercing gaze of Dana Reynolds. With her long nails and blood red lips, she looked like a vampire.

Jarli cleared his throat. 'Uh, hi. I saw your story about Red Ninja. It was . . . interesting.'

Reynolds wasn't so easily distracted. 'You never gave me that interview,' she said.

Reynolds was a TV journalist who had hounded Jarli relentlessly when he first released his app. More recently, she had helped him research Viper. He had promised her an interview in exchange.

'I can do the interview this weekend?' he offered weakly. He was missing too much school already.

'No good now,' Reynolds said. 'You released the app six months ago. Even your involvement with the plane crash was more than three months ago. You're old news, Jarli. Unless . . .' She looked him up and down. 'Tell me, what exactly are you doing here?'

'Uh, I'm not sure I'm allowed to say.'

Reynolds' eyes widened. 'Reeeaaally?'

'Gotta go,' Jarli stammered, and turned towards the building.

'Wait.' Reynolds grabbed his arm with a

manicured claw. 'An anonymous source just gave me some interesting information. After the press conference tomorrow, I'd love to get your take.'

Jarli felt increasingly uncomfortable. 'I'll see if I'm allowed.'

'You shouldn't need permission to do the right thing,' Reynolds called. But Jarli was already running towards the doors.

A porter and a security guard looked at him, then at each other, then at Jarli again, trying to work out who was supposed to greet him.

The security guard—a burly man with a ponytail—appeared to win this silent battle. 'Name?' he said gruffly.

'Uh, Jarli Durras,' Jarli said. He suddenly realised he didn't have any ID.

But the guard didn't ask for any. He pulled out his phone and used *Truth Premium* to confirm that Jarli wasn't lying.

'Stand still, please,' the guard said. He waved a metal detector wand over Jarli. It bleeped when it reached Jarli's pocket. Jarli pulled out his phone. The guard nodded. 'OK. You can go in.'

'May I take your bag, *sir?*' the porter asked, leaning too close to Jarli. He managed to make 'sir' sound like an insult. Jarli recognised him from school. Richie. He was older and had recently spray-painted swearwords and clumsy cartoons all over the side of the school gym. Everyone knew he'd done it, but they were too scared of him to say anything.

'No thanks,' Jarli said, not meeting his gaze.

Richie smirked, as though this was just what he had expected from a wimp like Jarli. He heaved on a brass handle and opened the glass doors. Jarli slipped through into the lobby.

A few important-looking people in suits and expensive jewellery were walking around, but Jarli couldn't see Agent Lindsay anywhere. Maybe Jarli had misunderstood the driver's instructions. She might have meant Lindsay would meet him in the lobby tomorrow, before the press conference.

Jarli approached the reception desk. The young blonde woman behind the counter smiled at him.

'Uh, hi,' Jarli said. 'My name's Jarli Durras. I'm supposed to check in.'

The woman discreetly checked her phone to make sure he was telling the truth. 'Welcome to the hotel, Mr Durras.'

Everyone used *Truth Premium* for everything now. Whoever stole Jarli's app must have made a fortune before they started giving it away as a free download. Jarli sometimes wondered why they had done that. Maybe to kill off Jarli's own app, which hardly anyone used anymore.

The woman handed Jarli a plastic square.

'Is this my room key?' Jarli asked.

'No.' The woman took the plastic square back. 'You open your room with your thumbprint.'

Jarli was more and more confused. 'Do you have my thumbprint on file?'

The woman dropped the plastic square into a slot. Her computer beeped.

'We do now,' she said, beaming. 'You're in Room 404. It's in this building, on the fourth floor. Just so you know, the fifth floor is off-limits—the conference VIPs are up there.'

She wrote on a card and gave it to Jarli.

'Uh, thanks.' Jarli took the card, wandered into one of the lifts, and pushed a button for the fourth floor. The highly polished mirrors on either side reflected infinite Jarlis, stretching away into eventual darkness.

Ding! The doors opened, revealing the fourth floor. Lush carpet, dim downlights and oil paintings throughout.

Jarli couldn't find Room 404, which struck him as funny. When a browser can't find a website, it's called a 404 error. He paused in the corridor and took a photo of the card with his room number on it so he could post a joke about it on social media. Then he realised it probably wasn't a good idea to tell the internet which room he was in.

He put his phone back in his pocket but didn't delete the photo. He could make a post about it tomorrow, when he had left the hotel and it was safe to give away the location.

Finally, there it was—Room 404, tucked around the corner next to the fire stairs. He pressed his thumb against the sensor pad. It bleeped and a green light flashed. Jarli pushed the door open—it seemed to weigh a tonne—and slipped inside.

Wow. Jarli walked into the room, eyes wide. The bed was huge, with a mattress twice as thick as Jarli's one at home. Four ornate antique lamps cast a warm yellow glow across the lush carpet. There were huge windows and a spacious balcony overlooking the courtyard between the two curved buildings of the hotel. Judging by the thick tube of fibre-optic cables connecting them, there was probably really fast internet here. Being a technology expert, Kellin Plowman must have insisted on that when building his golf resort.

Jarli could see movement through one of the windows in the opposite building. Sellick, the assistant minister, was unpacking her suitcases on her bed. Her room was on the same level as Jarli's. He felt a bit sorry for her—like him, the assistant minister wasn't considered important enough for the top floor.

Jarli closed the semi-transparent curtains and checked out his bathroom. It had a huge marble bathtub and big mirrors, recently polished. He wondered how much it cost to stay here. Was this the most luxurious hotel in the world, or did it just seem that way because he lived in Kelton? He couldn't believe Plowman owned all this. He must be loaded. The five-thousand dollar prize for the Robattle suddenly seemed insignificant.

Jarli didn't notice the TV right away. In sleep mode, the screen was exactly the same shade as the wall. He woke it up and scrolled through the options.

Every movie or TV show he could think of was here.

He took off his jacket, sat on the edge of the bed and sent a text to Bess.

So the rooms at the golf resort are surprisingly great.

Her response was immediate.

I'm not jealous. Nope, not at all.

The government people said charges to the room were covered. You want to come here and hang out? We could get room service and watch Darth Vader not being a robot.

Have mercy. I have homework to do. Remember?

Jarli cringed. He'd forgotten that he was supposed to be helping Bess with her science project right now.

I'm sorry, but I don't think I can come over to help you out with that.

Yeah, I figured. ☹

Maybe Anya could help? I think she gets good grades in science.

They can't be worse than mine. I'll text her.

Originally from somewhere in Russia, Anya was a year ahead of Jarli and Bess at school. She and Jarli had done gymnastics together for school sport last term, while Bess's parents had made her try fencing. Now that Jarli thought about it, he hadn't seen Anya much since then. He had thought they would stay friends after escaping from Cobra together, but maybe Anya had decided it wasn't cool to hang out with younger kids.

The hotel room suddenly seemed lifeless and suffocating. The thought of ordering room service and watching a movie without Bess made him feel guilty, so he left the room and went back downstairs.

The main foyer was even busier now. Staff were

buzzing back and forth, polishing things which already looked shiny. More security guards had appeared, their radios beeping and burbling.

Jarli wondered if he was allowed to leave. Sellick and Lindsay had implied that he would be here the whole time. But the conference wasn't until tomorrow, and there was nothing to do. Jarli didn't even like golf.

He sank into a couch, not far from a lanky businessman who was hunched over his phone. When he sat down, the businessman moved away.

Vaguely offended, Jarli pulled out his own phone. He sent a message to Anya:

Hey, how are you? Haven't seen you around much lately. I was wondering if you could help Bess with her chemistry project?

She heated lead oxide with carbon in class, and now she's supposed to work out how much carbon dioxide was produced. I said I'd help, but now I can't.

Busy

Jarli was startled. Anya had always seemed friendly and helpful.

OK, thanks anyway. What are you up to?

Not safe to talk on the phone.

Jarli stared down at the screen. He didn't understand what was going on, and if he couldn't use his phone, he didn't know how to find out.

As Jarli looked up, trying work out what to do, he saw a commotion outside. The journalists were taking pictures of a man getting out of a car. When the crowd parted, he recognised Aaron Fisher from the TV. The Minister for Defence.

Jarli had never seen him in person. He was a tall man with silver hair and a regal nose. He wore a grey suit which Jarli could somehow tell was expensive.

Fisher stopped outside the front of the hotel to make a brief speech. Sellick stood slightly behind him, one step higher so they looked equally tall. Two bodyguards stood nearby, but no sign of Agent Lindsay. This struck Jarli as odd, since Lindsay had said he was the head of ministerial security, or something like that.

Jarli did see one more person he recognised, though. Irena Blanco, the suspended constable, lurking up the back of the crowd.

The glass was too thick for Jarli to hear the grumble of the reporters, but Fisher's commanding voice was audible:

'It's an honour to be opening the TwentyTech Conference. I look forward to many productive discussions with our corporate partners and international allies over the next two days. I just wish there was time to squeeze in a round of golf.'

None of the journalists laughed, but they all looked satisfied with that soundbite. All except for Dana Reynolds.

Reynolds held up a microphone—the foam top blazing orange like a firebrand—and opened her mouth to speak. Jarli couldn't hear her voice, but version three of his *Truth* app had a lip-reading function. Bess had been helping him test it. He pointed the camera at the window just in time to catch the second half of Reynolds's sentence.

Words appeared on the screen: >. . . RESPOND TO THE ALLEGATIONS OF FALSE INTELLIGENCE?

'It wouldn't be polite for me to comment on my own intelligence,' Fisher boomed.

No-one laughed, and Reynolds persisted.

>SOURCES ALLEGE----

'No further questions.' Fisher turned away, blocking Jarli's line of sight to Reynolds.

Jarli was starting to realise why he had been invited to appear at this conference. It wasn't just a 'demonstration of openness.' He was here to deflect a particular accusation.

Sellick, Fisher and his entourage entered the hotel through the revolving door. Reynolds and a few other journalists tried to follow them, but the security guard with the ponytail stopped them.

Fisher walked past Jarli towards the reception desk. A smell of aftershave and styling mousse caught Jarli's nose.

Wondering what Reynolds had been accusing him of, Jarli did a quick search on his phone.

Search: *Aaron Fisher false intelligence*

He found what he was looking for right away.

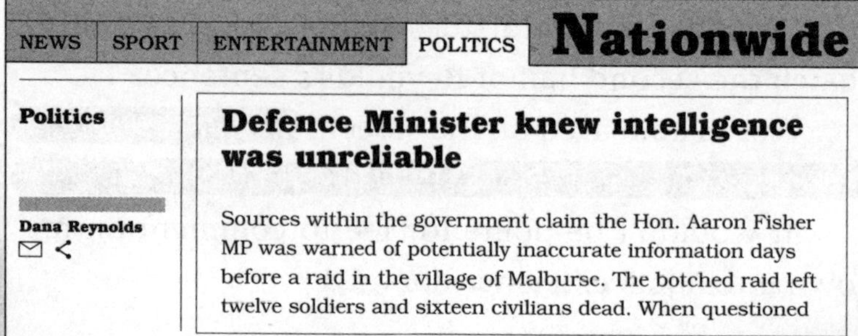

NEWS | SPORT | ENTERTAINMENT | POLITICS

Nationwide

Politics

Dana Reynolds

Defence Minister knew intelligence was unreliable

Sources within the government claim the Hon. Aaron Fisher MP was warned of potentially inaccurate information days before a raid in the village of Malbursc. The botched raid left twelve soldiers and sixteen civilians dead. When questioned

Jarli skimmed the rest of the article. The raid was five years ago, but the accusations about Fisher were new.

The accusations must be untrue, though, Jarli thought. *Otherwise he wouldn't want me to use my app on him. Or maybe he's just not going to talk about that?*

Jarli spotted Agent Lindsay outside, pushing through the crowd of journalists. The man flashed his ID and said something to the security guard. The security guard waved the metal detector over Lindsay, who held up a phone and a ring of keys. The guard let him through the glass doors into the lobby. Lindsay spotted Fisher's entourage near the counter and started walking towards them.

Jarli stood up. 'Agent Lindsay!'

The agent looked around, but didn't seem to notice Jarli until he waved. Jarli ran over.

'What do you want?' Lindsay's voice sounded hoarse compared to what it had been yesterday. Maybe he had spent the night shouting at someone.

'I'm not sure what to do,' Jarli said. 'Can I leave the hotel and come back, or do I have to hang around until the conference?'

'You'll have to sort out your own problems, kid,' Lindsay said. 'I'm not a babysitter. I'm the head of ministerial security.'

Jarli was confused. The driver had told him that Lindsay would give him instructions. And it sounded like Lindsay didn't even recognise him.

And then Jarli's phone beeped. LIE

Jarli and Lindsay stared at each other for a split second. Long enough for Jarli to realise that Lindsay wasn't really the head of security. Maybe he wasn't even really Lindsay. His voice did sound different, and Jarli thought his eyes were a different shade.

The impostor had heard the beep too. He reached into his pocket.

Jarli opened his mouth to yell to the security guards—

And then the imposter slashed at Jarli's throat with his keys.

'Hey!' Jarli jumped backwards, instinctively.

One of the keys skimmed the fabric of his T-shirt, slicing through it and nicking the skin beneath. These weren't ordinary keys. They had been sharpened into blades.

Jarli backed away, out of range. 'Hey,' he shouted again, loudly enough to get the attention of everyone in the room.

The imposter swung the keys again—

But someone grabbed his wrist. One of Fisher's security personnel. She was a round-faced woman with curly hair and a lanyard which said CLARKE.

'William,' she said. 'What are you doing?'

'Activate blackout mode,' the imposter said.

And then all the lights went out.

BLACKOUT MODE

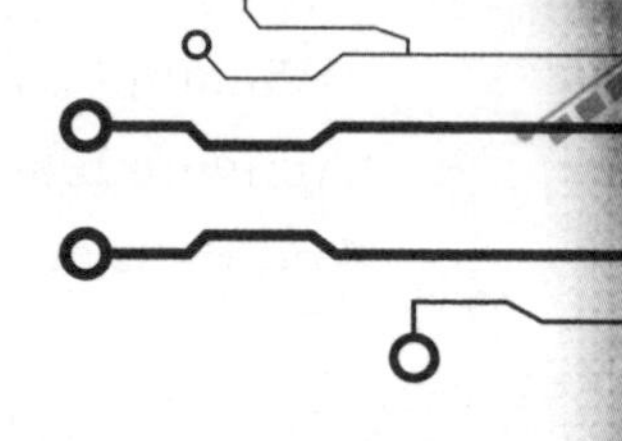

Screams filled the room as security shutters rolled out over the windows and doors, eliminating the natural light. It wasn't pitch-black—thin gaps in the shutters still cast stripes of light across the carpet—but Jarli and the impostor were in darkness. Jarli ducked, afraid that the imposter would take another swing at him with those sharpened keys.

He didn't. As Jarli's eyes adjusted to the darkness, he saw that the imposter had wrestled free of Clarke's grip and was charging at a terrified Fisher. When he got close enough, he stabbed at Fisher's neck—

But Clarke tackled the imposter. The keys missed Fisher's throat by centimetres.

All the other bodyguards were in action now, hustling Fisher and Sellick towards the exit.

'What's happening?' Sellick demanded as she was herded away. She didn't look as frightened as Fisher had. 'How many hostiles?'

No-one answered her. Fisher himself was almost invisible now—just a flash of silver hair in the huddle.

'You're under arrest,' Clarke was saying. She had the imposter pinned to the floor, but she hadn't cuffed him yet.

'Activate smoke grenade,' the imposter said.

Bang! Something exploded in the impostor's pocket. The noise was so loud it made Jarli dizzy. A cloud of thick smoke billowed out, swallowing the imposter and Clarke. One of the other security guards had finally managed to deactivate the shutters, but the sunlight that came flooding in couldn't penetrate the smoke. The cloud was spreading and no-one could see.

Jarli started running towards the entrance. He wasn't alone. Everyone seemed to be doing that, except for the hotel security guards. The area was packed with screaming guests and panicked-looking hotel staff. To make matters worse, the journalists outside were instinctively drawn towards the danger, and desperately trying to get in. They pushed and forced their way into the revolving door. It was spinning with so much force that Jarli was worried he might get crushed.

But he couldn't turn back. There were people pushing on either side of him and from behind. He was getting railroaded towards the revolving door.

Swoosh! One of the door panels rushed past as he approached. *Swoosh!* Again. And then—

Jarli threw himself into one of the compartments just in time to avoid getting smeared between the panel and the doorframe. But the revolving door spun him around so fast that he didn't have time to get outside. He found himself thrown back into the hotel, surrounded once again by panicked people and hungry journalists.

'Jarli!' Dana Reynolds grabbed him and dragged him out of the fray with one surprisingly strong hand. 'What's happened?'

'I, uh . . .' There was too much to explain, so nothing came out.

Dana squeezed his shoulder until it hurt. 'Get a grip. What's going on?'

'There was a man,' Jarli stammered. 'He said he was the head of security, but he was lying. And then—'

'Who?' Reynolds demanded. 'Where is he?'

Jarli looked around. The smoke was starting to clear. He could see Clarke, unconscious on the floor. But there was no sign of the impostor.

Horsham was taking the long route back to Throwaway. He'd changed into a tracksuit and dumped his business clothes, splitting them between three separate charity bins. The exploded remains of his phone were dissolving in a jar of ACID in one of the cup holders.

A police car appeared up ahead. Horsham gritted his teeth as it zoomed towards him, closer and closer—and then hurtled past, siren screaming.

Horsham exhaled. His gaze flicked to the rear-view mirror. That blue hatchback had been behind him for a while. He flicked his indicator on. The blue car didn't.

Horsham spun the wheel, taking the car down a narrow side street. The blue car went right past. They hadn't been following. Or, if they had, they'd realised he was onto them.

It was time to call Viper and admit he had failed. Horsham was terrified. But he couldn't put it off any longer. Viper would be watching the news. If he found out that way, the punishment would be death.

Horsham stopped the car again and pulled a burner phone out of the glove compartment. Several contact numbers were saved in it, all random. Dead ends to confuse the police. Horsham dialled a different number from memory.

The phone rang for only a second before Viper picked up.

The voice was distorted, but Horsham could hear the excitement in it. 'Is he dead?'

Horsham took a deep breath. 'No.'

There was a terrible scream of rage from the other end of the line, freezing Horsham's blood.

'OK,' Viper said, suddenly calm. 'Tell me what went wrong.'

'Let's start again,' Detective Arno said. 'You see the head of security acting suspiciously. You approach him—'

'No,' Jarli said. 'I didn't realise he was acting suspiciously. I approached him because I'd been told he would give me instructions.'

'Told by who?'

'My driver.' Jarli felt ridiculous saying this. Like a member of the super-rich.

They were sitting on chairs in the hotel lobby. Arno was tapping notes into a phone while Jarli talked. The lights were back on and other police officers were interviewing the staff and the journalists who had made it into the lobby before the impostor disappeared. A coffee van had pulled up outside and was making a fortune from the rest of the media.

Arno had straight hair and dark eyes which gave nothing away. She was the detective who had interviewed Jarli after Viper had tried to kill Doug's family. *Truth Premium* gave her an honesty score of 94%, but Jarli didn't completely trust her. One of the police officers he'd met in the past had turned out to be working for Viper. Another, Constable Blanco, was still suspended. Jarli had learned to be careful.

'And when you approached Lindsay,' Arno said, 'he attacked you with his keys?'

'I told you, it wasn't Lindsay. His voice was different. His eyes were a different colour. And when he said he was head of security, my app told me he was lying. That's when he attacked me.' It sounded less convincing every time Jarli said it. 'And he vanished right after.'

'Uh-huh,' Arno said. 'Did anyone else's phones go off?'

'No. Maybe no-one else was close enough,' Jarli said uncertainly. Plenty of people had been around, but this was the only explanation he could think of.

Arno leaned back in her chair. 'Your story is impossible,' she said.

'But—'

'When he arrived, he told the security guard outside the hotel that his name was William Lindsay. The security guard's app said he was telling the truth.'

'But . . .' Jarli trailed off, thinking. The guard,

like everyone else, had been using *Truth Premium*, the rip-off of Jarli's app. But Jarli had the original version on his phone.

'I'm using a different app to everyone else,' Jarli said.

'There you go,' Arno said. 'Yours must be unreliable.'

Jarli bristled. 'The other app is a knock-off of mine. *It* must be unreliable.'

'Uh-huh.' Arno stood up. 'You can go back to your hotel room. The conference is still going ahead—' She grimaced, and Jarli got the feeling she thought that was a bad idea. '—and I gather your participation is required. Don't worry, we'll catch Lindsay. We're watching his bank accounts, tracing his phone, and we have officers at his home.'

'It's not his home, though,' Jarli insisted. 'He's not the real Lindsay.'

But Arno was already walking away.

Cops bustled around the foyer, snapping photos. Hotel staff hovered anxiously nearby. No-one talked to Jarli, or even looked at him. He lay down on the couch, suddenly exhausted and feeling invisible. If only his parents were here. They would believe his version of events. They wouldn't think his app was unreliable—in fact, they usually complained that it was too accurate.

Some things should remain secret, Dad often said.

Jarli found himself looking up at a security camera in the ceiling. Would it have seen anything useful? Maybe not after the smoke bomb went off. But what about before that? It would have had a clear view of the impostor.

Jarli looked around the room. The receptionist was over by the door, talking to the police. No-one was behind the reception desk. The glow against the wall behind it told him that the computer was switched on.

Jarli stood up. He strolled over to the reception desk and stepped behind it as though he was allowed to. Bess did this all the time. With a little confidence, she seemed to get away with everything. She had once picked up the microphone at the school athletics carnival and started announcing events. No-one realised she wasn't supposed to be doing that until she summoned competitors for the 'hopping-backwards race'.

Once Jarli was behind the reception counter, he checked that no-one was looking his way, and then ducked out of sight. From this side, the desk looked much less glamorous. Sticky notes with passwords scrawled on them. Pens without lids. Spare rolls of receipt paper gathering dust next to the fingerprint machine which Jarli had seen earlier.

On the screen, Jarli could see the defence minister's booking.

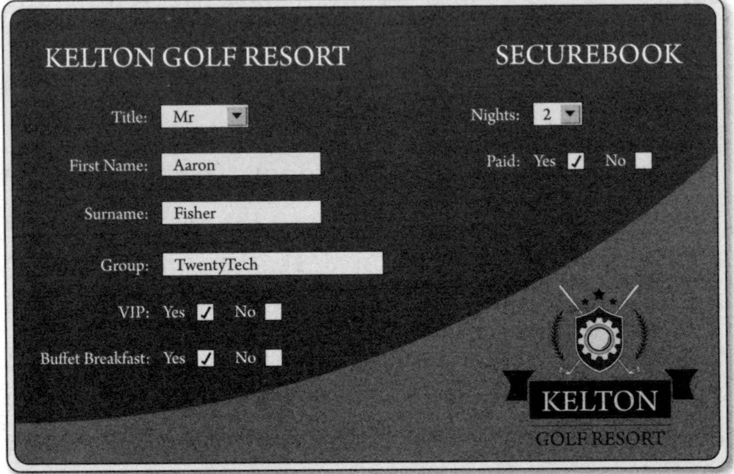

KELTON GOLF RESORT

SECUREBOOK

Title: Mr

First Name: Aaron

Surname: Fisher

Group: TwentyTech

VIP: Yes ✓ No

Buffet Breakfast: Yes ✓ No

Nights: 2

Paid: Yes ✓ No

Jarli brought up a search window and typed in, *CCTV*. No results. *Camera*. Too many results. *Surveillance*. Nothing.

When he typed in *security*, he found what he was looking for. The security-video program brought up a grid of camera feeds from in and around the hotel. Jarli couldn't see inside any of the rooms, but he could see every corridor, the restaurant, the roof . . .

. . . and the lobby. He could even see himself crouched behind the reception desk. Now he just needed to know how to rewind.

One of the voices got louder. Someone was coming. Jarli froze.

But it was OK. Whoever it was walked straight past the reception desk.

After a bit of fiddling Jarli realised that he could just click on the time code and type in a different time. Arno had grilled him about the time, so he knew exactly when the smoke bomb had gone off. He typed in *14:35:00.*

On the screen, he watched himself approach the impostor. There was no sound. It was nerve-wracking, even though he knew the end of the story. On-screen Jarli didn't realise that he was in danger.

The impostor mouthed the words, *blackout mode*. All the feeds went dead. The impostor had not only killed the lights, but the cameras too. Jarli wondered how this was possible. The impostor must have connected his phone to the hotel staff wi-fi, and then—

'Ahem.'

Jarli looked up. A bearded, man in a white hat stood behind the counter. His gold watch gleamed. Jarli guessed from his vest and tartan pants that he was probably a golfer. His face looked familiar, but Jarli couldn't place it right away.

'Uh, hi,' Jarli said, his heart racing. 'Welcome to the hotel. Do you, um, have a reservation?'

'My name is Kellin Plowman,' the man said. 'It's *my* hotel.'

Jarli gulped. 'Oh.'

'Give me one good reason why I shouldn't have you arrested.' Plowman gestured at all the police behind him. They weren't looking Jarli's way—yet.

'Because I'm one of your valued customers?' Jarli suggested weakly.

Plowman turned towards the police.

'No, wait!' Jarli said quickly. 'The police are looking for William Lindsay. But the guy who set off the smoke bomb wasn't the real William Lindsay. I talked to him, and my app caught him in a lie. That's why he attacked me.'

Plowman's eyes narrowed. 'You're Jarli Durras. We met yesterday.'

'Right.'

'And you just waltzed behind my reception desk and started reviewing security footage?'

Jarli cleared his throat. 'Well . . . yes.'

Plowman's face broke into a smile, showing the gap between his front teeth. 'I like your attitude, young man,' he said. 'Real innovators don't wait for permission. Let's see what you found.'

Shocked but relieved, Jarli shuffled over, making room for Plowman behind the desk.

'I haven't made much progress,' Jarli said, keeping his voice low so the other people in the lobby didn't overhear. 'The cameras went dead as soon as the lights turned off.'

'Yes.' Plowman was already looking at the screen. 'The mystery man hacked into my system, and I'm keen to find out how. Fortunately, there are other cameras.'

'I checked every feed in the hotel,' Jarli said.

'There are feeds outside the hotel.' Plowman brought up a program and typed in a sixteen-character password.

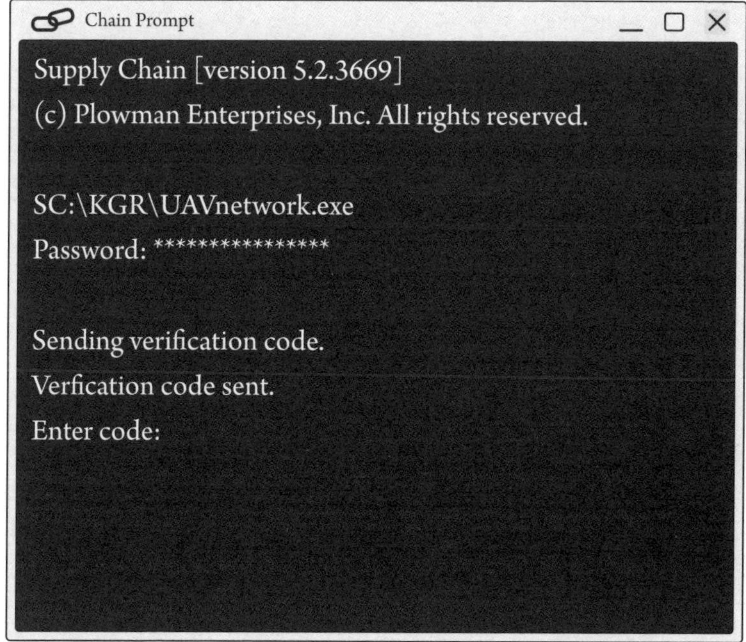

A moment later Plowman's phone beeped. He checked the screen and typed in a verification code.

'Shouldn't we, uh, tell the police what we're doing?' Jarli asked.

'Not my style,' Plowman said, looming over the screen. 'Check this out.'

MASS SURVEILLANCE

Jarli found himself watching the hotel from above. It rotated slowly, windows gleaming.

'You have a drone circling the hotel?' he said.

'Beyond the reach of our mystery man's hack,' Plowman said. 'And . . . '

He pressed another key. Other feeds popped up. The hospital. Kelton Town Hall. The police station. Jarli's school.

Jarli was aghast. 'You have drones circling the whole town?'

'Keep your voice down,' Plowman said, shooting a dark look at the nearest police officer, who was picking fibres off the carpet with a pair of tweezers. 'But yes, I do. They have night vision, infra-red, everything. And they're solar-powered, so they can fly around more or less indefinitely.'

'Is that legal?'

Plowman didn't seem to hear the question. He was fully absorbed by the computer. He brought up the footage from within the hotel, opened a module called FaceTrack, and highlighted the impostor's face. A progress bar appeared.

'Since there are so many cameras, I can only store the last 24 hours of each feed,' he told Jarli. 'But we should be able to figure out where the man who attacked you went after he left the hotel. The facial recognition algorithm tracks—'

A message popped up on the screen.

'Hmm.' Plowman opened a text log and started scrolling though. 'Here's the problem. According to the drone cameras, our mystery man was in two places at once this morning.'

'Or two people were walking around with the same face,' Jarli said slowly.

'Exactly.'

Jarli kept his voice down: 'We should tell the police.'

'No,' Plowman snapped. 'If they were serious about solving this crime, they would still be talking to you instead of play-acting for the media. There's every chance they're in cahoots with the criminals.'

He brought up the footage from the drone circling the hotel and typed in a new time code. The scene was suddenly chaotic—hotel staff trying to get out of the hotel, and media fighting to get in.

A box appeared around the head of a man running towards the car park. FaceTrack identified him as William Lindsay.

'There's our mystery man,' Plowman said. He switched to a feed from the car park. The impostor appeared, walked over to a red sedan and climbed in. As he drove away, Plowman highlighted the number plate **SNK-817.**

A new module popped up. *VehicleTrack*.

Plowman toggled a setting.

The screen flickered as the program fast-forwarded through all of Plowman's drone footage from the afternoon. A few times, Jarli spotted the red sedan. Usually it was moving, but sometimes it was parked by the side of a road. Eventually, the time code on the screen matched the clock on the wall. Just one video feed was playing now, and it showed the vehicle cruising down the highway in real time.

'Now we're getting somewhere,' Plowman said.

Plowman held up his phone next to the computer. Then he flicked the video feed from the monitor onto the phone screen, like a magic trick. Jarli boggled. Cameras, drones, computers, phones—he had never seen such a diverse network in action, and all so well-connected.

'Come on,' Plowman said, and started to walk across the lobby. People instinctively moved aside, including the police. No-one wanted to be in the rich man's way. Jarli followed him, wondering where they were going.

Plowman unlocked a back door and led Jarli out into the courtyard between the two buildings. An electric golf cart was parked on the grass.

'You'll have to drive,' Plowman said. 'So I can keep tracking him on the phone.'

'Wait,' Jarli said. 'What are we doing, exactly?'

'Catching the mystery man, of course. Looks like he's on his way back to town.' Plowman climbed into the passenger seat.

Jarli started to wonder if Plowman was losing his mind. 'You want to chase down a dangerous criminal . . . in a golf cart?'

'Of course,' Plowman said. 'I can't let a minor drive a proper car. Don't worry, the golf cart is quite fast. And it's an electric motor, so it's quiet too.'

'The guy must be nearly an hour's drive away,' Jarli objected.

'Yes, but he has to stay on the road. We don't. We just need to meet him at his destination. Hop in.' There was a dangerous glint in Plowman's eyes.

Jarli hesitated. Riding in a normal car was scary enough, since the crash. The golf cart had no doors, and only thin seatbelts. And Plowman's behaviour had gone beyond 'eccentric billionaire'. His tech skills were incredible, but that didn't mean he was in touch with reality. He was illegally monitoring the whole town. Was it safe to get in a vehicle with him?

'Hurry up!' Plowman said.

Reluctantly, Jarli climbed into the golf cart. He couldn't think of a better way to get answers.

There was no handbrake and no gearstick—just a switch marked *forwards* and *backwards*. The steel pedals and the little steering wheel brought back memories of the bumper cars at the Kelton Show. They weren't happy memories. Somehow, Jarli had always ended up facing backwards, pummelled by other cars. That was why he had wanted Sir Ramington to be autonomous—because Jarli knew he would have been a terrible driver.

Huge in the tiny vehicle, Plowman buckled his seatbelt. 'Let's go,' he said.

'How do I—'

Plowman turned a key—it was tiny, no bigger than the key to a bike lock—and the golf cart beeped. It was ready to go.

Cautiously, Jarli flicked the switch to *forwards* and eased his foot onto the accelerator. The golf cart started to roll forwards across the grass.

'Go that way,' Plowman said, pointing. 'Quick as you can.'

Jarli spun the wheel towards the golf course and floored the accelerator. The engine whined and the cart lurched forwards, zooming over the rolling hills at a terrifying speed. His teeth were chattering in time with the bouncing wheels.

Plowman kept his eyes on his phone. 'He has to stay on the roads,' he said. 'And he's caught a couple of red lights. So by the time we reach the road, we'll have gained on him by about six minutes. Not nearly enough to catch him. But if he stops somewhere in town—bunker. Bunker!'

A crater filled with sand appeared out of nowhere. Jarli spun the wheel just in time. The cart leaned as it hurtled around the edge of the sandpit, but didn't tumble in.

'Crikey,' Plowman said. 'Be careful!'

This was your crazy idea! Jarli wanted to scream. He gritted his teeth and said nothing as the golf cart rocketed over the course. It practically went airborne at the top of each hill.

'You may have started to suspect by now that I don't like golf,' Plowman said.

Jarli had suspected no such thing. 'What? You don't?'

'No. It's a ludicrous sport. But it's a good excuse to build a luxury hotel in an isolated spot.'

'Why did you want to do that?'

'I'm not paranoid,' Plowman said, sounding more paranoid than ever. 'But something is going on in this town.'

'Can you be more specific?' Jarli asked.

'I was working on a new kind of distributed data-storage system. I made a new kind of cryptographic hash function, which—'

'You mean Supply Chain,' Jarli said. About ten years ago, Plowman had released a free, easy-to-use video-editing program. As well as making videos, the software stored small chunks of encrypted data on the user's device. Since each chunk was replicated across many devices, it couldn't be modified or deleted, because Plowman's program would immediately notice and undo the change. Plowman made other free programs—games, email clients, antivirus tools—and soon he had half-a-billion users, all storing bits of data for him. This was the SUPPLY CHAIN—a vast reservoir of information, completely unhackable and as permanent as the internet itself. Plowman had licensed this platform to some cloud-computing companies and made a fortune.

Plowman nodded. 'I should have guessed you'd be familiar with it. Anyway, I can't see any of the data that goes into Supply Chain. Not without the login credentials of whoever put it in. But I can see where the data is coming from, and where it's going. A huge amount of it is flowing in and out of Kelton.'

'Really?' Jarli was surprised. Most of the adults he knew barely understood what a router was.

'My best guess is that it's cryptocurrency,' Plowman said. 'Hundreds of millions of dollars changing hands, right here in town. You know about cryptocurrencies?'

Jarli did. Cryptocurrencies were the cash of the online world—data used as money, anonymous and almost untraceable. But cryptocurrencies need secure online storage systems to work. Systems like Supply Chain.

Jarli raised his eyebrows. 'Who would be moving that kind of money in Kelton?'

'Other than me? No-one that I've been able to

find. Whoever is doing this is has gone to enormous trouble to stay hidden. I tried, but I couldn't break my own encryption. I couldn't see what the people were saying or doing. And I couldn't narrow down their exact location—just that they were within fifty kilometres of Kelton.'

The more Plowman talked, the more sick Jarli felt—and it wasn't just the bouncing of the golf cart.

Viper, he thought. *It has to be.*

'So I built this hotel,' Plowman continued. 'I thought that any visiting criminals—ultra rich ones—wouldn't want to stay at the crummy old Kelton motel. They'd prefer a place like this. Luxurious. Exclusive. But when they're at my hotel, I have a chance to observe them. Collect their fingerprints. X-ray their bags and their cars. Monitor their phone calls.'

'Why are you telling me all this?' Jarli asked.

'Because someone with something to hide,' Plowman said, 'wouldn't invent a lie-detector app. I looked into your program and it's the real deal. I know this is the first time we've met, Jarli—but I trust you more than anyone else in this town.'

Jarli's phone didn't beep. Plowman was telling the truth. But that didn't mean Jarli had to trust him in return.

'My app warned me that the minister's security

chief wasn't who he said he was,' Jarli said. 'But the police say it must be wrong, because otherwise everyone else's phones would have gone off.'

'Ah, but everyone else uses *Truth Premium*,' Plowman said knowingly.

Jarli felt a flush of pride. 'You're saying *Truth Premium* is less reliable than my app? I assumed the programmer just copy-pasted my code.'

'They did. Then they made modifications.'

Jarli knew that *Truth Premium* had a different interface, but he didn't think that was what Plowman meant. 'What kind of modifications?'

'I hacked into the software to see what the differences were,' Plowman said. 'It's programmed to ignore certain voice prints.'

'What do you mean?'

'I mean there are a few people the app always trusts, no matter what they say. I guess the imposter is one of them.'

A chill crawled up Jarli's spine. 'But . . . everyone uses *Truth Premium* now. Even more so now that it's free. The government, the police, the media . . .'

'Exactly. Imagine a criminal who can deny anything—or claim anything—and always be believed. Did I mention that *Truth Premium* also turns every phone into an audio surveillance device? It doesn't just listen to your conversations. It records them and sends them somewhere. I still haven't figured out where. They can also use the app to get inside your home wi-fi. What kind of firewall do you use?'

Jarli cleared his throat. 'Uh, I made my own, actually. It's called, um, WallOfFame.'

'Really?' Plowman looked intrigued. 'I guess that makes sense. You have some powerful enemies. Like—wait a minute.' Plowman was looking at the phone again, watching the recordings from his drones. 'He stopped.'

Jarli lifted his foot off the accelerator. 'He has? Where?'

'Don't slow down. He just pulled over on the side of the road, he's been there for a few minutes.'

'Maybe taking a phone call,' Jarli suggested.

'Maybe.' Plowman was silent for a moment. 'OK, he's on the move again. Still headed for the town centre.'

The cart was hurtling towards the edge of the golf course, which was surrounded by bushland.

'Through those trees,' Plowman said, pointing to a narrow trail.

Jarli hadn't liked driving over the golf course, but he liked the idea of driving through the bush even less. 'Isn't there a fence?' he wondered.

'Yes. We're going to ram it.'

'We're going to *what?*' Jarli couldn't spare a glance at Plowman to see if he was kidding. The golf cart was already bouncing up the trail, and it took all his focus not to crash into anything. His wrists ached from gripping the shuddering steering wheel.

'We're going to ram the fence,' Plowman said again. 'One section of it is built on a secret hinge. Pressure from the outside doesn't do anything, but pressure from the inside will knock it down.'

'Why did you build it like that?!'

'Look!' Plowman pointed at his phone. 'He's parked the car. And he's getting out this time.'

'Where?'

'Near the library.'

The chain-link fence appeared between the trees. It looked solid. It didn't look like the kind of fence that would fall over when rammed by a golf cart.

'Step on it!' Plowman yelled. 'If he's walking to his destination, we must be close.'

Jarli gritted his teeth and put his foot down.

The fence rushed up to meet them.

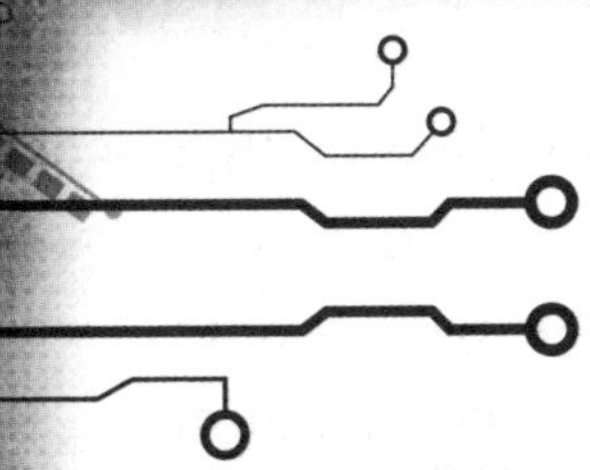

ZERO GRAVITY

Smash! The golf cart hit the fence—

And bounced backwards. Jarli was flung forwards. If not for the seatbelt, he would have hit the windscreen. The wire in the fence rattled, but the posts didn't budge.

'Whoops,' Plowman said. 'I must have forgotten to unlock it.'

'Are you kidding me?!' Jarli demanded. His neck and chest were killing him after the impact. His hands were trembling and sweaty on the steering wheel.

'Not to worry.' Plowman switched to another app on his phone and began entering a complicated passcode.

Jarli took a shallow, shaky breath. He didn't want to be here, in a golf cart in the bush with a crazy person. It was getting dark. He wanted to be at home, where it was safe, programming Doug's robot or helping Bess with her project.

I never fixed the wi-fi for Kirstie, he suddenly

realised. It was a strange thought to have at that particular moment. But what if he died out here and never got the chance? Maybe the wi-fi would become his unfinished business, and he could haunt it. Maybe the wi-fi was already HAUNTED, and that was why it rarely worked.

There was a sharp click. 'Got it,' Plowman said, and a section of the fence tilted over. It didn't fold flat—just to a 45-degree angle. The golf cart would have to drive over it like a ramp.

Plowman switched back to check VehicleTrack. 'Floor it,' he said.

Jarli hesitated. 'Can't we just walk over?'

'We'll never catch him if we leave the cart behind. Go, go!'

Jarli gripped the steering wheel and pushed down on the accelerator. The golf cart zoomed towards the fence.

'Faster,' Plowman said. 'We don't want to tip over forwards when we get to the top.'

This made Jarli want to slow down, but he forced himself to speed up instead. The cart hit the fence and shot up the slope, chains rattling under the tyres. When it got to the top it went airborne. Jarli's organs swam around in a second and a half of zero gravity, and then the wheels slammed down onto the weedy dirt on the other side of the fence.

Plowman cackled with glee. 'Nice driving, young man! When you hit the highway, turn left.'

Jarli took a deep breath and put the pedal to the metal again. If they didn't catch the mystery man, it was all for nothing.

'I don't understand,' Plowman said.

Jarli had parked the golf cart on the footpath in front of the public library. They had received some strange looks from pedestrians and other drivers, but no-one had objected out loud to seeing a golf cart driving around Kelton, not even as it went through red lights and bumped over train tracks. People seemed to recognise Plowman and his distinctive hat. *Rich people can get away with anything,* Jarli thought.

Plowman was staring at his phone. 'The guy parked his car just around the corner from here,' he said. 'The drone lost sight of him when he walked into an alley behind the library. But he didn't come out again. And the alley is a dead-end.'

Jarli remembered the alley. After running away from Kelton Town Hall yesterday, he had planned to hide in there. He felt a twinge of excitement. 'So he's still there?'

'I guess so—but that was ten minutes ago. What would he be doing in a blind alley for ten minutes?'

'Maybe it's time to call the police,' Jarli said, shivering as a cool breeze picked up in the street.

'They weren't interested in the mystery man before,' Plowman said. 'We haven't really learned anything new, so what makes you think they'll care now? No, Jarli, it's up to us to investigate!'

He clambered out of the golf cart, and Jarli reluctantly followed. They walked along the street, the library on their left, parked cars on their right. Jarli was chewing his lips so hard it hurt. It was hard to shake off the feeling that this was some kind of trap.

They reached the corner of the library and turned left into the alley.

It was too narrow for cars. The high brick walls and overlapping eaves blocked out all daylight. Small mushrooms flourished in the cracks where the ground met the walls. There were NO DOORS, NO WINDOWS.

And no people. The mystery man was gone.

'Impossible,' Plowman whispered. He turned around and around, scanning for the mystery man. Then he looked back down at his phone. 'Nothing has left this alley since he walked in. He should be here.'

Jarli crept up towards the other end of the alley, trampling a carpet of rotted cardboard and shredded plastic, looking for an escape route. He didn't find one. But there was a big dumpster on rusty wheels in the back corner. It looked abandoned—the alley was too narrow for a garbage truck.

'Mr Plowman?' Jarli said. His voice trembled a little. If the mystery man hadn't left, there was only one place he could be.

No sound. The dumpster was as quiet as a grave.

Plowman came over. 'Oh dear,' he said softly. 'Avert your eyes, boy. You probably shouldn't see this.'

Jarli stepped back and squeezed his eyes shut. He didn't want to be here, looking for a criminal in a smelly alley.

He heard the squeak of the dumpster's hinges. And then—

'Hmm,' Plowman said.

Jarli opened his eyes. Plowman didn't look like he'd spotted a dead body. When Jarli stepped forward, he saw that the dumpster was completely empty. No dead body. No rubbish, even.

'Curiouser and curiouser,' Plowman said.

PART TWO: BATTLE

THE APP WAS SUPPOSED TO MAKE EVERYBODY MORE HONEST. I THOUGHT PEOPLE WOULD BE LESS LIKELY TO LIE IF THEY WERE MORE LIKELY TO GET CAUGHT. BUT I WAS WRONG—THE STATS SAY THAT DISHONESTY HAS ACTUALLY INCREASED. I GUESS YOU'RE MORE LIKELY TO LIE IF YOU KNOW EVERYBODY ELSE IS DOING IT TOO.

—From the documentation for Truth, *version 3.2*

ACT NATURAL

The next morning

Jarli glared at the enormous toaster. It was a bizarre design; slices of bread were carried slowly along a conveyor belt while heating elements did precisely nothing, and then ejected it from the bottom, uncooked. Jarli had put his bread through twice already, and it still hadn't transformed into toast. Why couldn't this place have a normal toaster?

Jarli might have handled this challenge better on another day. But right now he was exhausted. The bed in his room had been soft, but it wasn't his bed. Little things had woken him up several times in the night. The humming of the mini-fridge. A door closing somewhere else in the building. The frame of light around his curtains, coming from a floodlight in the courtyard below. Eventually he had given up and watched TV until sunrise.

The toaster spat out his bread, somehow burned to a crisp.

'Hey, kid.'

Jarli turned around to see the driver who had dropped him off at the hotel yesterday. She looked well-rested and alert, in a pristine navy suit. *Fresh as a daisy,* Mum would have said.

Jarli had talked to his parents last night. They had seen the attack on the news. For once, Dad hadn't sounded too anxious. And Kirstie was delighted by the whole thing—she was working on some theory that the imposter had been an evil clone of the real head of security. But Mum was worried enough for all three of them. Jarli had found himself reassuring her, pretending it hadn't been that dangerous.

'The speech is in an hour,' the driver said. 'But they need you upstairs now. Conference Room D.'

'I haven't had breakfast yet,' Jarli said.

A pyramid of apples stood in a nearby bowl. The driver plucked one from the top and tossed it to Jarli. 'Eat on the way,' she said.

Dazed, Jarli turned and started walking towards the lifts. When he looked back, he saw that the driver was already gone. A waiter was balancing a new apple on top of the pyramid.

'You just have to stand right here, holding up your phone,' Sellick was saying. 'The journalists will be seated over there. Don't do anything else, don't move off your mark and don't say anything to the reporters or anyone else. Don't smile—that will look too staged. But don't look suspicious either. Just act natural.'

Act natural, Jarli thought. It seemed impossible.

Conference Room D was huge, with plenty of high-backed chairs, dozens of water decanters and a huge smartboard dominating one wall. A lectern had been set up next to it, thin microphones wobbling like alien antennae as the hotel staff adjusted it.

Kellin Plowman was in the corner, shaking hands and patting backs with three men and two women in expensive suits. Jarli guessed that they were the tech leaders who were presenting at the conference. He reminded himself that Plowman had built the hotel just to spy on people. No doubt he was keeping a close eye on them.

Jarli didn't make eye contact with him. After they drove back to the hotel last night, they had agreed not to meet again in public.

A security technician was fitting some kind of intricate mesh to the windows overlooking the golf course. Maybe she was making the glass bulletproof.

'What if there's another attack?' Jarli asked Sellick.

'There won't be.'

'But what if there is?'

'We've tripled security.'

'Well, yesterday a guy who looked a lot like the head of security tried to kill me,' Jarli said. 'And your boss.'

Sellick glared at him. 'You want to bail out? There'll be no fee if you do.'

Jarli thought of his mum, and all extra hours she was working. 'No,' he grumbled. 'I'm still in.'

'Thrilled to hear it.'

Jarli noticed that Sellick had a microphone fixed to her lapel. 'Do I need one of those?' he asked.

'No.' Sellick was adjusting Jarli's collar, as though it were school-photo day. 'You're not making a speech.'

'What if someone asks me a question?'

'There will be no questions. Especially not for you. The journalists have been told to keep their mouths shut until the end of the conference when they can ask all the questions they like.'

Jarli remembered the scrum of reporters outside the hotel yesterday. Fisher's answer to Reynolds's question: *It wouldn't be polite for me to comment on my own intelligence.*

Jarli's app worked by analysing choice of words, tone of voice and pupil dilation using the phone's built-in camera. This could determine if the person was nervous, or thinking hard, or using evasive language. A combination of all three usually meant the person was lying.

But by making a confident, well-rehearsed statement, Fisher had avoided triggering any alarms. Jarli wondered how he could reprogram the app to solve that problem.

Sellick adjusted her jacket. It was bulky, and Jarli realised there was a bulletproof vest beneath it.

'Where's *my* bulletproof vest?' Jarli asked.

'You don't need one. You're not the assistant minister.'

Jarli looked uneasily at the bullet-proof mesh now covering the windows.

'No-one's going to be shooting,' Sellick said. 'It's basically an insurance thing.'

Jarli's app didn't go off. But just because she wasn't lying, that didn't mean she was right.

The Honourable Aaron Fisher MP breezed into the room, flanked by even more security guards. There were now a lot of people in the conference room, and there was only one small door. *If a fire alarm goes off,* Jarli thought, *I could get trampled to death.*

The Minister for Defence looked cheerful for someone who had recently survived an assassination attempt. Maybe he had been watching the news.

Jarli had seen on the TV that the attack had actually boosted Fisher's popularity.

The minister's cool blue eyes scanned the room, and settled on Jarli. After a split-second pause, a smile lit up his face.

'You must be Jarli Durras,' he said, extending a hand.

Jarli shook it. The minister's grip crushed his fingers.

'Uh, yeah,' Jarli said. 'Nice to meet you.'

A moment later he worried that his phone would beep, embarrassing him. But the phone let him get away with it, this time. He must not have sounded as nervous as he felt.

'Excuse me.' Sellick walked away, snapping her fingers to get the attention of some security guards.

'Thank you for taking the time out of your busy schedule to do this,' Fisher's voice seemed to fill the whole room.

'I'm not that busy,' Jarli said.

'You're a high-school student! I'm sure you're almost as busy as me.' Fisher laughed, as jolly as Santa, while a security operative tightened the straps of his body armour.

'Well, thank you for inviting me,' Jarli mumbled.

'To be honest—which I'm sure suits you—it was Norma's idea. But I'm pleased to have you on board.'

Jarli glanced over at Sellick. She had given Jarli the impression that it was Fisher who wanted him here.

Another security person had finished attaching a microphone to Fisher's lapel. 'You're good to go, sir.'

'Thank you, Hank.' Fisher picked up a glass from the table and took a sip of water. 'Pro-tip, Jarli—always drink some warm water before a speech. Loosens up the vocal cords. Are you ready for this?'

'Yes,' Jarli said.

His phone beeped.

Fisher laughed again. 'Well, at least we know your app's working. Oh, here they come!'

Journalists had started to stream through the door, accompanied by camera operators and sound technicians. Fisher stood behind the lectern as they took their seats. Sellick joined him. Jarli stood next to them both, his mouth dry.

A woman with a head-set mic led the journalists to their seats. Jarli did a double-take when he realised it was the stage manager from the Robattle. Kelton probably didn't have many event managers.

'After the minister's address there will be a ten-minute photo opportunity,' she was saying, 'followed by refreshments in the courtyard around the back of the building. There will be no questions.'

Jarli saw that Dana Reynolds had managed to get a seat right up the front. Fisher flashed her an insincere smile.

Sellick nudged Jarli. 'Get your phone out.'

Jarli pulled the phone out of his pocket with shaking hands, brought up the *Truth* app, and held the phone in front of the minister.

'We need to see the screen,' someone whispered.

Jarli hurriedly turned the phone around to face the reporters.

When everyone was seated, Fisher raised his hands, and a hush fell. 'Ladies and gentlemen,' he said. 'Thank you all for coming. It's my great privilege to be a part of the TwentyTech Conference. Shortly I will introduce some of the esteemed delegates who . . .'

Jarli had already tuned out. He found himself looking at a printout of Fisher's speech sitting on the lectern. Large font, wide margins, double spacing. Someone had written all over it with blue pen. Fisher barely glanced at it as he spoke. The speech looked long. They could be here for hours.

' . . . Jarli Durras,' Fisher continued, and Jarli snapped to attention, 'is the inventor of the *Truth* app, and a role model for today's youth. He's using his app on all of us right now. This conference is about using technology to promote peace, at home and abroad. Peace requires trust, and all parties have agreed to Jarli's presence—a testament to the trust we have with our allies.'

'Mr Fisher,' someone said.

Jarli's heart sank when he saw that Dana Reynolds had raised her hand. He should have known that she would take 'no questions' as a challenge.

Security guards started to move in from the corners of the room.

'There will be no questions today,' Fisher said.

'Fourteen children have gone missing from police custody over the last five months,' Reynolds said. 'Can you comment?'

Unease flashed across Fisher's face. 'I'm not familiar with . . .'

He stopped, but it was too late.

Jarli's phone beeped. LIE

Everyone looked at it.

Reynolds smiled. 'I'm sorry, Minister. What are you not familiar with?'

'There will be no questions,' Fisher said again.

One of the security guards had grabbed Reynolds, but she was still talking. 'Senior sources within your own government allege that you ordered children—'

'If your question is about police custody,' Fisher said, 'it would be best directed to the police commissioner.'

The phone beeped again. What Fisher had said might have been true, but Jarli's app could tell that he was rattled, and speaking evasively. Jarli wondered if he should turn the phone off, or if that would make things look even worse.

The smiles were fading from the faces of the delegates.

'Fourteen children are missing,' Reynolds said again. 'My sources say that some of them had been exposed to classified information, or had witnessed events which the Department of deemed—'

A vein stood out on Fisher's forehead. 'Get her out of here.'

The security guards were already dragging Reynolds away, but the other reporters smelled blood in the water.

'Mr Fisher!' someone yelled. 'What do you know about these missing kids?'

'Mr Fisher!' someone else shouted. 'What would you say to the families of—'

'Mr Fisher! Why did—'

The minister muttered something Jarli didn't catch and turned away from the crowd. Suddenly his security team was on the move. Half were hustling Fisher and the delegates out of the room, while the other half held back the reporters. Jarli found himself pushed towards the door.

'I want that woman arrested,' the minister hissed to an aide as soon as they were out in the corridor.

The aide looked uncomfortable. 'The press has certain legal rights—'

'In that case, I want her press pass revoked. I want every other journalist running stories about every bad thing anyone has ever accused Reynolds of doing. *Then* I want her arrested.'

The friendly, genial man Jarli had met earlier had vanished. Fisher had turned orange, bright spots of colour burning on his cheeks.

Cameras clicked back near the conference room door. Some reporters had made it past the security guards.

Fisher barged through a fire door into a stairwell, crushing dead moths under his polished loafers. Jarli hesitated. Was he supposed to be following?

As if he could sense Jarli's hesitation, the minister turned around. His face was fixed in a forgiving smile, for the cameras outside. But Jarli could see the fury in his eyes.

'Sir,' Jarli said. 'I don't know what's going on.'

'I said nothing untrue,' Fisher said, through gritted teeth. 'Your app is defective.'

'What? No,' Jarli stammered. 'It uses nervousness as—'

'You won't be paid for coming today. I'll make

sure that everyone knows this is all your fault.'

Jarli's mouth fell open. 'You can't do that!'

'You've made a powerful enemy.' Fisher strode away up the stairs, leaving Jarli feeling sick and alone.

Jarli's phone was ringing. The screen said *Mum*.

Oh no, the money, Jarli thought. Now he couldn't help her with the bills.

'Hi, Mum,' he croaked, answering the call.

'Hi, sweetie,' Mum said. 'Are you OK?'

'Yeah.' Jarli's phone beeped, and he heard hers do the same.

'It wasn't that bad,' Mum said. Two more beeps. Jarli realised she had been watching the speech live. 'I mean, the minister came off much worse than you.'

'He's not happy,' Jarli heard himself say as he stumbled towards the lifts. His legs felt weak.

'I don't care about him. I care about you.'

Jarli didn't want to be cared about. He wanted to disappear.

'It won't be like last time,' Mum continued. 'All the heat will be on him.'

'I was standing right next to him.'

'Yes, you're visible in the footage. But you know what the only good thing about the twenty-four-hour news cycle is?'

'Endless commentary instead of news?'

'Stories disappear *fast,*' Mum said, ignoring him. 'Just come home and wait it out. People will have moved onto the next thing before you know it. There'll be another royal wedding or something.'

Jarli didn't think it would be that simple. But he was already at his hotel room, somehow. He could pack his things, go back downstairs and check out. *At least it's over,* he told himself. *I can be out of here in five minutes.*

'OK,' he said. 'Can you come pick me up? No, wait. Send Bess's mum.' Jarli didn't want his mother devoured by the media hoard. Bess's mum owned a taxi company. She would appreciate the publicity. 'I don't know how we'll get past the reporters, but—'

'We'll think of something,' Mum promised.

After he hung up, Jarli started packing his things. It didn't take long. Yesterday's clothes were on the floor. His bathroom bag was beside the sink. His phone charger was plugged into the wall. That was it.

Jarli turned around, doing one last sweep of the room, and saw the envelope on his bed.

The envelope hadn't been there when he left this morning. Someone had been in his room.

The bed wasn't made. Not housekeeping. So, who? Plowman, maybe?

Jarli picked up the envelope. Squeezed it. Nothing hard inside.

He was about to tear it open when he realised it wasn't sealed. A single sheet of paper was folded inside. The text was printed, not handwritten.

> Jarli,
>
> Please excuse the invasion of your privacy. Other forms of communication can be intercepted. You're in danger. We both are.
>
> Don't trust anyone, especially the defence minister. Meet me in Room 502, as soon as possible, and I'll explain everything.

He read the words over and over. Should he tell someone? The letter had told him not to, but he didn't necessarily trust the sender. Unfortunately, none of the people he did trust were here. He couldn't call Bess, or Doug, or his parents. *Other forms of communication can be intercepted.*

If somebody wanted to hurt him, there were easier ways. And if they wanted to deceive him, they wouldn't have asked to meet in person. His app worked better on a human being than on a piece of paper. Leaving the note behind, Jarli walked out the door and headed for the lift.

As he rode to the top floor, he glanced up at the camera bubble in the ceiling. *Plowman will see this, if he looks. That means I'm safe. Right?*

He emerged from the lift on the top floor. The corridor was identical to the one below, which made the room easy to find. It was almost directly above Jarli's.

Jarli took a deep breath and knocked on the door.

No answer.

He knocked again. The door shifted slightly. It was unlocked.

No, propped open. A pen lay on the floor, stopping the door from closing all the way.

Jarli knocked again and pushed the door partly open. 'Hello?' he called.

NO ANSWER. He couldn't see anything through the gap, so he pushed the door open wider, slipped through, and picked up the pen so the door could close.

The room was a copy of his own, like a clone from a parallel universe. Big windows looking out over the courtyard to the curved building opposite. A soft bed, unmade.

There was a broken vase on the floor at the foot of the bed. Jarli walked closer, and picked up one of the thick shards of pottery. It was heavy and strong. It wouldn't have shattered unless it had hit something hard. Had someone knocked it over? But Jarli's room had the same vase perched in the bathroom. Nowhere near the bed.

Then Jarli saw the foot.

It was bare and hairy, with toenails going white at the edges. It stuck out from behind the bed like one of the chew toys that Jarli's dog was always leaving behind.

Holding in a scream, Jarli edged around the bed to see a body in a hotel bathrobe, sprawled on the carpet.

Because of the blood, it took Jarli a minute to recognise the man's face. It was Agent William Lindsay.

RAT IN A TRAP

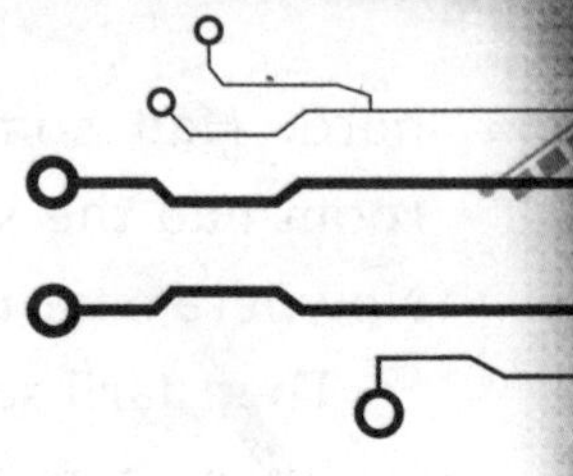

Jarli stood paralysed for almost a minute. Should he check for a pulse? Lindsay sure looked dead. His eyes were half-open, and only the whites were visible. What if touching the body counted as interfering with evidence? And was this the real William Lindsay, or the impostor?

I have to call someone, Jarli thought. But the letter had said not to trust anybody. Especially not the defence minister, and most of the security here worked for him.

If the letter was from Lindsay, it looked like he, too, had trusted the wrong person.

Eventually Jarli decided that *not* calling the cops would make him an accessory. So he dug out his phone with shaking hands and called triple 0.

The woman picked up quickly. 'Police, fire or ambulance?'

'Uh, ambulance,' Jarli heard himself say. 'And police. I'm in Room 502 at the golf resort in Kelton. I don't know the address.'

He was surprised by how calm he sounded. It was like his brain was divided in two. The talking part and the panicking part, kept separate.

The woman was reading out Jarli's mobile number. 'Is that the right number to reach you on?' she said.

Jarli was confused. 'Where are you going?'

'In case I lose you,' the woman said. 'Is that your best contact number if I need to call you back?'

'Oh. Yes.' Jarli stared down at the body. 'I think he's dead.'

'Who is?'

'Uh, a guy named William Lindsay. He worked for the government.'

'Are you alone?'

'What?'

'Are you alone in the hotel room?'

Jarli whirled around. He hadn't checked the rest of the hotel room. 'I'm not sure,' he whispered.

'Can you repeat that?'

Jarli didn't. The bathroom door was closed. Jarli stood as still as a tombstone, listening. He couldn't hear anyone moving in there.

'Are you still there?' the woman asked.

Cautiously, Jarli reached for the doorhandle. He turned it, pushed the door open and leapt back, just in case something swung out of the darkness.

Nothing did. As Jarli's eyes adjusted to the shadows within, he saw what looked like an empty bathroom.

'Hello?' the woman said.

Jarli crept inside, and peered behind the door. A towel hung from a hook. Nothing else. Jarli checked the bath. No-one hiding in it.

'I think I'm alone,' he said finally.

'OK. That's good. Stay where you are. Police are already on their way.'

Jarli noticed that the closet door was slightly ajar. A rectangle of darkness stretched from the top to the bottom. He couldn't see in. But if anyone were inside, they would be able to see out.

He eased over to the closet, as silently as a shark. Reached for the door with a trembling hand. Flung it open.

There was a bathrobe on a hanger, and an ironing board. Nothing else.

'Tell me more about the man,' the woman said. 'Are you sure he's dead? Have you checked his pulse?'

Jarli was about to reply when something flashed outside the window. Lightning, or a camera flash. He peered through the thick glass. What was that?

There was no-one in the courtyard below. Jarli couldn't see anyone in the opposite building—the balconies were all empty, and so were the few rooms with open curtains.

Then something moved on the roof.

Jarli squinted. It was definitely a person with a camera set up on a tripod. The figure wore a black ski mask.

Whoever it was, they had been watching this room.

Jarli's phone beeped. Another call was coming through. He checked the screen. Kellin Plowman. Last night, Plowman had said 'no calls'—they would communicate via encrypted messages only. Why would he be calling now?

'I've gotta go,' Jarli said, and ended the emergency call before the woman could object. Then he answered Plowman's call. 'Hello?'

'Jarli,' Plowman said urgently. 'Someone's coming to get you.'

'What? What are you talking about?'

'You're in Room 502, right? I was looking at the cameras and I saw you going in. Then I saw six people going up the stairs towards you. Four more went into the lifts and pushed the button for the fifth floor. Five others are blocking the downstairs exits.'

'That'll be the police,' Jarli said. 'I just called them.'

'They don't look like police. They look like private

security, but they're not with me. You've got to get out of there now. Soon you'll be trapped.'

Jarli looked down at Lindsay's body, his mind whirling. His app thought Plowman was telling the truth. And, now that he thought about it, he knew the police couldn't have got here so quickly. So who were the people on their way to the fifth floor? And what would they do if they caught Jarli in Room 502?

Jarli decided not to find out. Keeping the phone to his ear, he ran out the door into the corridor.

He was too late. He could hear footsteps coming from his right. Somewhere to his left, he heard the ding of a lift arriving.

'They've reached the fifth floor!' Plowman hissed.

Jarli ran back into Room 502 and closed the door. He locked it and engaged the chain. That would keep them out for a while. But would it last until the police arrived?

A knock at the door. 'Open up,' a male voice commanded. He didn't identify himself. He didn't say 'police'.

Frantically, Jarli looked around for somewhere to hide. But he had searched the hotel room a minute ago. He knew all the hiding places, and none of them would conceal him for long.

A fist pounded the door. 'We know you're in there.'

As quietly as possible, Jarli rolled the sliding door open and stepped out onto the balcony. A wall of cold air hit him. There were two chairs and a small table out here, but nowhere to hide.

He drew the curtains and closed the balcony door. Then he peered over the railing and immediately felt DIZZY. It was a long drop to the paved courtyard between the two buildings of the hotel, and there was no way to climb down.

A thud from the front door, rattling the hinges. Someone was trying to kick it in.

Above Jarli's head, swinging in the breeze, was the heavy-duty internet cable connecting the two buildings.

Jarli's heart rate went through the roof. He had a choice—use the cable to climb across the courtyard to the opposite building, or wait here until someone broke the door down and found him on the balcony.

He pocketed the phone, climbed onto the tabletop and reached for the cable.

BASE JUMPING

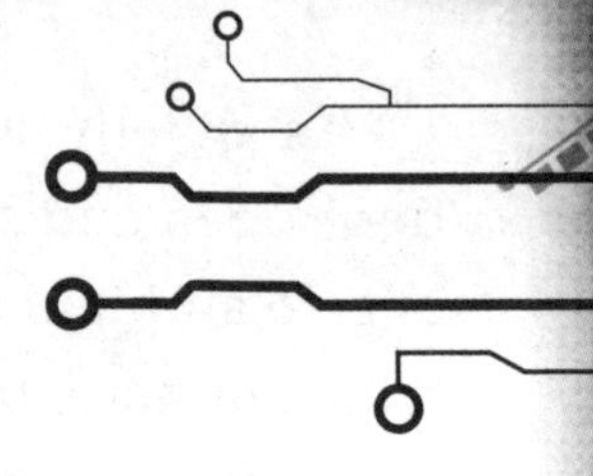

The internet cable was slightly out of reach. Jarli had to jump off the table to grab it. The table toppled over and crashed down onto the balcony.

The voices outside the front door of the hotel room went silent. Whoever was out there was listening.

Smooth rubber coated the cable. It would get slippery when Jarli started to sweat. Maybe this was a bad idea.

He looked behind him, through a gap in the curtains. The front door had been unlocked somehow and opened as far as the chain would allow. The door shuddered as someone kicked it again. Jarli knew it was only a matter of time before the hinges gave out or the chain broke.

Gritting his teeth, he swung his legs up and wrapped them around the cable like he'd seen Anya do at school. The cable sagged under Jarli's weight, but didn't break. Feeling more confident, he started wriggling towards the other building, like an upside-down caterpillar.

Anya had made this look easy. She could scale a rope like a monkey. But Jarli's progress was painfully slow, especially with the cable swaying in the wind.

The void yawned underneath him. It was a long way down. If Jarli lost his grip, he would be splattered against the paved courtyard below.

Don't think about it, he told himself.

By the time he was halfway across, his shoulders burned, his hands were trembling and sweaty. The rubber felt hot. This had been a terrible idea. But it was too late to go back.

Another gust of wind buffeted him sideways. Jarli held on tight with both hands, squeezing his eyes shut. The cable swung back and forth like a trapeze.

Something creaked behind him.

Jarli opened his eyes and looked back the way he'd come. The cable was attached to a big transformer. Sparks were shooting out of it. The connection wasn't designed to take Jarli's weight. It might snap!

Jarli panicked. He released his legs, hanging from just his arms. Then he swung from one hand to the next like he was on the monkey bars, moving away from the sputtering transformer as fast as he could. Soon he was only ten metres away from the opposite rooftop. Now nine. Eight. Every swing was agony in his arms. Seven. His lungs ached. Six. But he was going to make it. Five. Nearly there—

With a sound like a cracking whip, the cable came loose from the transformer.

Jarli screamed as he swung the last few metres, like Tarzan on a vine. He crashed into the rail of the top-floor balcony.

Now the transformer on this building was taking all his weight. *CRACK!* The other end of the cable snapped.

Jarli let go of the cable and threw out a desperate hand—

And just managed to catch hold of the railing.

The severed cable fell past him, crackling like a sparkler. It hit the ground far below and coiled itself up like a serpent.

Jarli gripped the rail with both hands and dragged himself over it onto the balcony. He lay on his back for a second, his heart racing.

I nearly died, he thought. And then: *Half the hotel just lost its internet. Plowman's gonna be mad.*

He offered up a silent prayer of thanks to anyone who happened to be listening, and scrambled to his feet. He tried the balcony door, but it was locked. He couldn't get into the hotel room. But maybe he could get up onto the roof, where there was an entrance to the stairwell.

Jarli stood on the table and jumped, grabbing the edge of the rooftop. With quivering arms, he hauled himself up over the gutter.

The mysterious figure in the ski mask was still here.

The rooftop was lined with solar panels, water tanks and radio receivers. The masked figure—a woman, Jarli thought—stood on the far side of the rooftop holding a duffel bag. She also wore a backpack. There was a door marked **FIRE STAIRS,** but she was nowhere near it.

For a minute, Jarli wondered if this was the same person Doug had seen. But there was no red scarf, and this woman looked like an adult, not a teenager.

'Hey,' Jarli said. He was still out of breath. He had to resist the urge to spit.

The woman looked at him, her face inscrutable behind the ski mask.

'Did you see what happened to that man?' Jarli asked. 'In the hotel room?'

The woman said nothing.

Jarli took a step closer to her. She took a step back. But she couldn't go much further without falling off the other side of the roof.

'Someone attacked him,' Jarli said. 'Did you see who else was in there, before I got there?'

The woman still didn't reply. Maybe she didn't

want to get caught out by Jarli's app. It couldn't do anything with silence.

Jarli pulled his phone out of his pocket, to show her he was turning it off—

Then the woman turned around and threw herself off the rooftop.

Jarli gasped. He ran, weaving through solar panels and air circulators, until he stood at the opposite edge of the roof, overlooking the golf course. He peered over, hoping he would see a balcony, and not another dead body far below.

He saw neither. The woman was soaring away under a black silk parachute. As Jarli watched, her feet skimmed a grassy hill halfway across the golf course. Then she detached herself from the backpack and dive-rolled to make her landing. The parachute settled like a plastic bag blown into a gutter.

Jarli wasted a few seconds watching the woman collect the parachute. Then he ran to the fire stairs and pushed through the door. He ran down flight after flight of concrete stairs, his feet a blur, sliding one hand along the bannister so he could grip it if he tripped.

He was almost at the ground floor when the alarms went off—a harsh beeping, and a recorded voice: 'Emergency. Stand by for instructions. Emergency. Stand by . . .'

Maybe the police had arrived. Or maybe Plowman was alerting his own security team to the intruders outside Room 502. Either way, the woman who had parachuted off the roof felt like the key to untangling this whole mess. Jarli hoped there was still time to catch up to her.

The recorded message changed. 'Please evacuate the building and proceed to the car park. This is not a drill. Please evacuate the building . . .'

Jarli burst out of the stairwell onto the ground floor. It was different from the one in the other building. There was a wide corridor with signs pointing to a day spa, a gym and—

The golf course. Jarli followed the signs to a glass door, and sprinted out into the daylight.

The woman was GONE.

Jarli sheltered his eyes with his hands, scanning the distant trees . . .

And saw movement. There she was, climbing over the chain-link fence.

Jarli sprinted across the grassy hills. Out the corner of his eye he saw the people hurrying out of the hotel buildings, heading towards the car park. Evacuating. Red and blue lights flashed—the cops were there.

Jarli's breathing was ragged. His whole body hurt. He wondered if it was possible to die from trying to run too fast. When he was a kid, Mum had read a book to him about a horse who ran too far without stopping and nearly died.

He heard Mum's voice now. *You're fine. Don't be a wuss.*

Jarli reached the fence. The woman was already gone. He needed to know who she was and what she'd seen. Jarli scrambled over the fence, the chain links digging into his fingers, and hit the ground on the other side. His legs wobbled from exhaustion. But he kept running.

As he ran towards the freeway, he heard a clattering sound in the distance. A train. Only two trains stopped in Kelton each day. Was it just coincidence that one of them was arriving now, or had the mysterious woman planned it this way? Maybe she intended to escape on that train.

Jarli caught sight of the woman again, sprinting towards the train station. He stopped at the edge of the freeway, waiting for a semi-trailer to zoom past. The rush of air almost sucked him into its wake as he ran across the asphalt.

Kelton Station was an old brick building with a ticket office that always seemed to be closed, toilets that always seemed to be locked, and a vending machine that was perpetually out of order. The train swept into the station, a huge aluminium tube with hissing brakes and scratched windows.

The woman ran across the tracks, jumped up onto the platform, and disappeared behind the train.

Jarli put on an extra burst of speed. He crossed the tracks, his feet scrunching through the pebbles in the railbed, and clambered up onto the platform.

Passengers flooded out of the train while others tried to cram themselves in, creating a human traffic jam. With only two trains per day, no-one wanted to miss out. Jarli scanned the crowd for the woman. He couldn't see her. He ran to the other side of the building, checking the other platform. Not there either.

He ran back to the train and pushed his way inside. About a third of the seats were full. Passengers shuffled through the aisle, dragging suitcases. Jarli looked around, but he couldn't see the mysterious woman in black.

The train's horn honked. The brakes hissed again. 'Doors closing,' said a recorded voice. 'Please stand clear.'

Jarli hesitated. There were other carriages to search. Should he stay on board, or get off and call the police?

Before he could decide, the doors slid shut and the train started to move.

ARMED AND DANGEROUS

As the train accelerated out of Kelton Station, Jarli worked his way up the carriage. He moved slowly, unsure if the woman knew he was on board. He didn't want to call attention to himself.

Most of the travellers looked tired—scruffy hair, bags under their eyes. One man was asleep against the window, snoring.

The woman had probably taken off her ski mask and maybe her black jacket, too. She might even have ditched the backpack at the train station. So Jarli wasn't exactly sure what he supposed to be looking for.

Recognition, maybe. When the woman saw him, she would react. Jarli just needed to pay close attention.

There were several women here. Any of them could have been the one he was looking for. He scanned their faces as he walked past, looking for suspect expressions. He compared their eyes to the ones he'd seen through the holes in the ski mask.

Dark and cunning, with thick lashes.

He pulled out his phone to tell Plowman what was going on. But the call wasn't active anymore. Plowman must have hung up.

The phone rang in Jarli's hand, making him jump. An unfamiliar number appeared on the screen. Jarli's phone automatically searched the web and identified it: *Kelton Police*.

'Oi,' a woman said. 'Quiet carriage, mate.' She pointed to a sign that read: THIS IS A QUIET CARRIAGE. PLEASE KEEP VOLUME TO A MINIMUM.

'Sorry,' Jarli mumbled, and went through the door at the end of the carriage. A noisy chamber with flexible rubber walls separated the quiet carriage from the next one. The floor swivelled under him as the train curved around a bend. Through the gap between the floor and the rubber walls, Jarli could see the tracks flying past. He opened another door to go into the next carriage.

He took a quick look at the passengers, wondering if one of them was the mystery woman. No-one looked alarmed to see him.

He answered the phone.

'Hello?'

'Jarli Durras?' said a voice. 'This is Detective Zee Arno, with the Kelton Police. Where are you?'

'I'm on a train,' Jarli said. 'To . . .' He tried to

remember the name of the next station in this direction. 'Axe Falls. Should be there soon. Why?'

'We need to talk to you,' Arno said. 'About an attempted homicide. We'll send someone to Axe Falls station to pick you up.'

'Attempted murder? Lindsay isn't dead?' Jarli felt relieved, and then guilty. He had been so sure that the man in the hotel room was dead. He hadn't even checked for a pulse.

'Not yet. The doctors think he might pull through. You got any idea what he's going to tell us if he wakes up?'

'What do you mean?'

'I mean that it might be in your interest to tell us what happened first.'

A blanket of unease settled over Jarli.

'I don't know,' he said. 'When I walked in, I saw his body—and a shattered vase, I saw that first—and I thought he was dead. Then I saw a flash from the opposite building . . .'

His phone beeped. A text message from Doug.

Dude! Turn on the news.

Another one came through immediately.

You're wanted for murder.

'You were saying?' Arno said.

'I'm the one who called you guys,' Jarli said. 'I didn't kill him.'

A few passengers looked up at him. Others deliberately avoided his gaze.

'I found him like that,' Jarli said. 'Check your app. I'm telling the truth.'

'Glad to hear it. Just turn yourself in, and we'll get this sorted out.'

Another message, this time from Bess.

Jarli! What's going on?

She'd attached a link to a news article.

SECURITY CHIEF ASSAULTED AT TECH CONFERENCE

In a second message, she attached another link:

TRUTH BOY WANTED FOR ATTEMPTED MURDER.

'I have to go,' Jarli said.

'I'd prefer it if you stayed on the line,' Arno said.

Jarli hung up and scrolled through the articles.

NEWS | SPORT | ENTERTAINMENT | POLITICS **Nationwide**

News

Jason Butcher

TRUTH BOY WANTED FOR ATTEMPTED MURDER

A police manhunt is under way for fourteen-year old Jarli Durras, who is suspected of assaulting William Lindsay at a hotel in the rural town of Kelton. Lindsay, the head of ministerial security at the TwentyTech Conference, went missing yesterday after witnesses say he attempted to attack the Hon. Aaron Fisher MP, Minister for Defence. Police say that Durras is armed and dangerous, and should not be approached.

Jarli's hair was standing on end. This was all wrong.

Another message from Doug:

They're saying you're armed and dangerous. That means they can shoot you on sight.

Jarli's thumbs quivered as he typed back:

I didn't do anything!

Ditch your phone. They'll have a warrant to track it soon.

Jarli was reluctant to do that. Without his phone, he would be completely on his own. He couldn't even follow the news to see what was happening.

But Doug was right. The police wouldn't have any trouble tracking him. And why would they have described him as armed and dangerous? He decided to just turn the phone off.

No-one except Jarli had seen the MYSTERIOUS woman in black. He had no proof that she had ever existed.

Don't trust anybody, the note had said.

Brakes squeaked, and Jarli stumbled sideways as the train started to slow down. It was way too soon—they couldn't have reached Axe Falls yet.

The driver's voice crackled over the PA system. 'Ladies and gentlemen, we apologise for this unexpected delay. We've been asked to halt the train here. We'll let you know as soon as we have more information.'

As the train got slower and slower, Jarli saw flashing lights out the window. The squealing of brakes faded, and soon he could hear wailing sirens. The police were coming for him.

Jarli hurried back the way he'd come, towards the quiet carriage. As he moved, the screen of another passenger's tablet caught his eye. There was a picture of Jarli at the press conference, next to another headline:

VIOLENT CRIMINAL ON THE LOOSE IN KELTON.

Jarli kept his head down, feeling conspicuous. This was a nightmare. If Doug was right, the police might shoot him on sight. He had to hide.

He pushed through the door into the noisy chamber between the two carriages and paused. No-one else was in here. But as soon as the train stopped, the police would board.

And the train was stopping right now. Jarli watched the tracks through the gap between the floor and the rubber wall as the wheels ground to a halt.

This gave him an idea.

Jarli crouched down, peering through the gap. It wasn't wide enough, but the rubber wall was flexible. He pushed his legs through. Grease slicked his palms and his jeans as they rubbed against the edges of the floor.

He heard doors opening in another carriage. Police were boarding the train. He had to hurry.

Jarli squeezed the rest of the way through the gap and fell onto the tracks. The gravel crackled beneath his shoes.

He looked between huge steel wheels and saw police cars parked next to the other side of the train. But no-one was on this side. There was a gravel slope down to some weedy grass and then a rickety wooden fence, separating the railway line from the farmland beyond.

Jarli slid sideways down the slope. When he got to the bottom, he realised he would be visible from the windows of the train. He risked a glance up. He could see some of the passengers, but they were all facing the other way, towards the flashing lights of the police car.

Jarli jumped over the fence and landed in the long grass. It was tempting to sprint across the paddock towards the bush in the distance. But he'd be visible the whole way. Someone on the train was bound to look out the window towards the paddock eventually.

Instead, Jarli crawled, slowly enough that the movement of the long grass would be camouflaged by the breeze. Soon his knees were dirty and his palms were raw.

When it felt like he had been crawling for hours, he heard the train hiss. He looked back, and saw that he had only gone thirty or forty metres. The train started to chug along the rails towards Axe Falls. The police car was already driving away. They must have searched the train, and concluded that he wasn't on it.

But soon they would track his phone. They would realise that the signal dead-ended at a spot on the line halfway between Kelton and Axe Falls. They would come back to search the surrounding area. Doug was right—he should have ditched the phone on the train instead of turning it off. It could have drawn the police away.

Jarli stood up and dusted himself off. The train was out of sight. The police cars were gone. It was just him, an empty paddock, and the afternoon sun dipping towards the horizon.

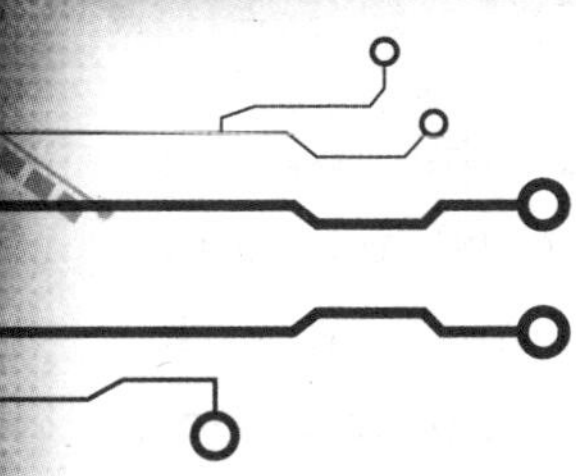

LOTS OF FOURS AND ZEROES

Dana Reynolds stormed into the Kelton police station like a hurricane of hairspray, perfume and questions. 'Detective Arno,' she said.

Arno glanced up from the mess of paperwork on her desk. She wondered if there was a way to get rid of Reynolds without giving her even more ammunition for her next story about police incompetence or corruption.

Probably not.

'Can you tell me why your officers have a shoot-to-kill order on a teenage boy who hasn't been charged with any crime?' Reynolds demanded. She levelled a microphone at Arno's throat like a sword.

Arno silently vowed to fire whichever moron had let Reynolds into the station. 'We've given no such order,' she said. 'Please leave so I can continue my investigation.'

'You released a statement saying he was armed and dangerous,' Reynolds said. 'Doesn't that effectively give police officers the right to shoot him?'

'The law is more complicated than that, as you would be well aware. And, for the record, we can't formally charge him until we arrest him, but Jarli Durras is wanted for assault with a deadly weapon. You might want to think twice before you leap to his defence.'

'When I studied journalism, I remember hearing about something called "presumption of innocence",' Reynolds said. 'Funny that they don't teach that in police school.'

'Your colleagues don't seem to care about presumption of innocence,' Arno said. 'They're all running stories about how Durras is a public menace, based on very few facts.'

She had tried to keep her voice neutral, but Reynolds must have heard something in it. A hint that they were actually on the same side.

'OK,' the journalist said, and put the microphone away. 'Give me some more facts, then. Off the record.'

Arno leaned back in her chair, wondering how much to reveal. 'Jarli Durras fled the scene, but we have Jarli's fingerprints all over the room,' she said finally. 'And on the weapon.'

'You mean the smashed vase?' Reynolds asked.

Arno sighed. 'Care to tell me how you know about that?'

'I never reveal a source. If the weapon was the vase, now smashed, then how can Jarli be considered armed and dangerous?'

'We have a witness who saw Jarli enter the room with a knife in his hand. We think the vase was an opportunistic murder weapon. The knife wasn't at the scene, so we have to assume he still has it.'

'What witness?'

'Nice try,' Arno said. 'I'm not going to let you pester them.'

'And the motive? Why would Durras attack Lindsay?'

'A document was recovered from the hotel room.'

'Which document?'

Arno said nothing.

'Off the record,' Reynolds persisted.

Arno shook her head. 'To tell you anything more would risk compromising the investigation.'

'How is the defence minister taking all this?'

Arno almost told Reynolds how much pressure she was under from the ministry. To bring Jarli in quickly, no matter what. It would have been a relief to share the burden with someone.

'He'll make his own statement, I'm sure,' she said instead.

It was getting dark, and cold. Jarli was just in his shirt, thin jacket and jeans. He might survive one night out in the bush, maybe. But no longer. So he started walking, just for warmth, stomping his numb feet through the undergrowth, sticking close to the trees for shelter from the wind. He soon found himself back in the outskirts of Kelton.

He crouched in some bushes near an empty playground. A woman was walking her dog. Jarli kept perfectly still until she had vanished down a path between two fences.

He couldn't switch on his phone to contact anyone, and he couldn't go to his house. The police would be watching it. His only hope was to stay out of their hands until they caught the real attacker. Hopefully Lindsay would wake up and tell them who it was. But was the unconcious man the real Lindsay, or the fake one?

In the meantime, Jarli needed somewhere to hide. Somewhere out of the cold, ideally with a computer so he could keep track of the case and find out when it was safe to come out of hiding.

He started walking towards the Kelton library.

The library had recently been rebuilt. Now it had the orange walls tilted at crazy angles, like it was collapsing in on itself. Old people had complained, but Jarli thought it looked cool, especially compared to the featureless grey building next door. The library was open until 9 p.m. on Fridays—that would give Jarli some time to figure out his next move.

He was walking towards the sliding doors when he spotted a silhouette on a nearby rooftop. A crouching figure. Jarli thought the person was looking at him, but it was hard to be sure—their face was hidden by a dark red scarf.

The Red Ninja, Jarli thought.

Before he could decide what to do, the ninja leapt off the rooftop. She caught a drainpipe and swung sideways, landing on a narrow windowsill. Then she quickly climbed down the wall, finding invisible handholds. In seconds she was on the ground, running towards Jarli.

Jarli backed away, looking around for an escape route.

'Jarli,' the ninja hissed. 'It's me!'

Jarli stared. 'Anya?!'

Anya nodded, but didn't take off the scarf. 'We can't talk here,' she said. 'Follow me.'

Jarli ran after her as she circled around to the other side of the library. There was a supermarket across the street with a steep roof. After a short run-up, Anya leapt off a park bench, caught the edge of the rooftop and pulled herself up out of sight.

Jarli wondered whether Anya thought he was

capable of doing that. He was just about to call out when a rope was thrown over the edge. Jarli grabbed the end and tugged it to make sure it was sturdy. Then he walked up the wall as Anya pulled the rope.

On the roof, Anya was holding a skylight open. 'In here,' she said.

Jarli climbed down into the darkness.

The roof cavity was small, and insulation foam made it deathly quiet. A battery-powered light shaped like a duck illuminated a camping mattress, a bucket, a journal, a first-aid kit and some bottled water. A telescope was mounted in one corner. A roof tile had been removed so the telescope could see out.

'What is this place?' Jarli asked, astonished.

'The war room.'

Anya had once told him she had secrets she would lie to protect. Maybe this was one of them. 'Are you fighting a war?'

'Not yet.' Anya gestured to the mattress. 'Take a seat.'

Jarli sat down, suddenly realising how exhausted he was. 'I didn't even know you were back from your boxing tournament.'

'There was no boxing tournament,' Anya said. 'I have been here the whole time.'

'Why?' Jarli looked around the gloomy roof

cavity. 'What have you been doing?'

'What have *you* been doing?' Anya said. 'The news says you are a murderer.'

It took Jarli a few minutes to explain the chaos of the last few days, jumping back or skipping ahead when he realised he'd left out something important. Anya waited in silence, not even nodding to show that she was listening.

'It sounds like you are short of both friends and enemies,' she said when Jarli finished.

'Short of enemies?'

'Yes. It is better to have an enemy than to be faced by a group of people whose allegiances are unknown.' Anya had a Russian accent, but Jarli often felt like she spoke English better than he did.

'My enemy is Viper,' Jarli said.

'But who is Viper?' Anya said. 'And who is Viper's enemy? I do not think it is you. Or at least, it is not mainly you.'

'Are you gonna tell me why you're hiding in a supermarket attic?' Jarli asked. 'Or why you've been walking around with a scarf over your face?'

Anya walked over to the telescope. 'Look at this.'

Jarli stood up and peered through the lens. He had thought the telescope was pointed at the library, but it was actually pointing at the boring grey building next door.

'Do you know what that building is?' Anya asked.

'The one next to the library? No.'

'I have been asking everyone,' Anya said. 'This is a small town. I thought someone must have the answer. Is it an apartment building? A hotel? A company office? A government office? But no-one knows. Or if they do, they are unwilling to say.'

'You could knock on the door and ask,' Jarli said.

'It does not have a door,' Anya said.

Jarli squinted through the telescope. Anya was right. The other side of the building was out of sight, but he didn't remember seeing an entrance there, either.

'The bank across the street has a door,' Anya said, 'and a suspicious amount of foot traffic. My best guess is that a tunnel under the street connects the two buildings, and that everyone who enters the mystery building does so via the bank.'

'But . . . why not just have a door?' Jarli wondered.

'If the mystery building had security shutters, cameras and guards all around it,' Anya said, 'people might have questions. But a bank is expected to have those things.'

The longer Jarli looked at the mystery building, the more it seemed to have an aura of MENACE. He took his eye away from the telescope. 'So what do you think they're doing in there?'

'I have been trying to find out,' Anya said. 'The building is owned by a company which is owned by another company which is owned by another company. The names are just jumbles of random letters. So I investigated in person. I covered my face so the cameras could not identify me. I watched at night, from trees and rooftops. At first I was trying to see through the windows, but now I think the windows are fake. The glass is just covering the concrete. So I started watching the bank instead, taking note of who comes and goes. And recently I saw something . . . worrying.'

'What?'

'It was just after 1 a.m. A black van arrived at the bank. It drove around to the back, where the money trucks are unloaded. But this was no money truck. Two armed guards got out. They opened the back of the van and took out a stretcher. There was a boy on it. He was shouting.'

'Was he hurt?' Jarli asked, eyes wide.

'Not that I could see. I think he was screaming for help.' Anya didn't meet Jarli's eye. 'They took him into the bank. And then I didn't see him again. I watched the bank all night, and most of the following day. He did not come back out.'

'Have you told the police?' Jarli asked. 'Or your parents? Do they know you're doing this?'

'I did not trust the police. So I contacted the journalist who helped you once before.'

'Dana Reynolds.' Jarli remembered her question at the press conference. *Fourteen children have gone missing from police custody over the last five months. Can you comment?*

It had sounded like Reynolds knew more than Anya had told her. She must have another source as well.

'Why didn't you tell *me?*' Jarli asked.

'Viper could still be watching you,' Anya said. 'The less you knew, the safer you were. As my father always says, it is hard to keep a secret these days.'

This phrase sounded familiar to Jarli, but he couldn't remember where he had heard it. 'How is this connected to Agent Lindsay?' he asked. 'Or the guy who was pretending to be him?'

'I don't know. Perhaps it is not.' Anya turned back to the telescope and kept watching the building. 'This is too big for us to tackle alone. Is there anyone else you trust?'

Not Plowman, Jarli thought. *Not the government. Not even the police.*

'Can I use your phone?' Jarli asked. 'The cops will start tracking mine if I switch it on.'

'Here.' Anya unlocked her phone and passed it to Jarli.

Jarli had memorised his parents' phone numbers, but he couldn't call them. The police might be listening at their end. He wondered what his mum and dad had been told, and whether they believed it. They wouldn't think he had attacked Lindsay . . . would they?

The only other number he knew off by heart was Doug's. It had lots of fours and zeroes, so it was easy to remember. Jarli dialled.

The phone rang and rang. Jarli found himself squeezing the receiver until the plastic creaked. Would Doug pick up?

'Hello?' Doug said finally.

'Doug. Thank goodness.'

'Jarli! Where are you? Everyone's looking for you.'

'Listen,' Jarli said. 'I didn't do what they're saying I did.'

'I know that.' Doug sounded offended. 'Any idiot can see that someone's setting you up.'

'I need—' Jarli hesitated as his brain caught up with his mouth. He had been thinking of this as a misunderstanding. It hadn't occurred to him that someone might be deliberately framing him.

If they were, he was in even worse trouble than he'd thought.

'I need a change of clothes,' he said. 'And

somewhere to hide. Can I come to your place?'

'Sure. But you'll need to climb over the back fence. I'll turn off the security light so Mum and Dad don't see you.'

'OK. See you in thirty minutes.'

As Jarli ended the call, he saw that Anya had left one of Dana Reynold's social media profiles open. A new video had been posted within the last few minutes. He tapped it.

'This is your seven o'clock news update,' Dana Reynolds said, her hands folded on her desk. 'A statewide manhunt is underway for Jarli Durras, the fourteen-year old suspect in the attempted murder of security operative William Lindsay.'

Jarli tried to shrink into his shirt, like a tortoise retracting its head.

'Police have described him as armed and dangerous,' Reynolds was saying. 'More on this story after the break.'

Jarli couldn't believe Reynolds had sold him out.

He remembered the note: *Don't trust anyone.*

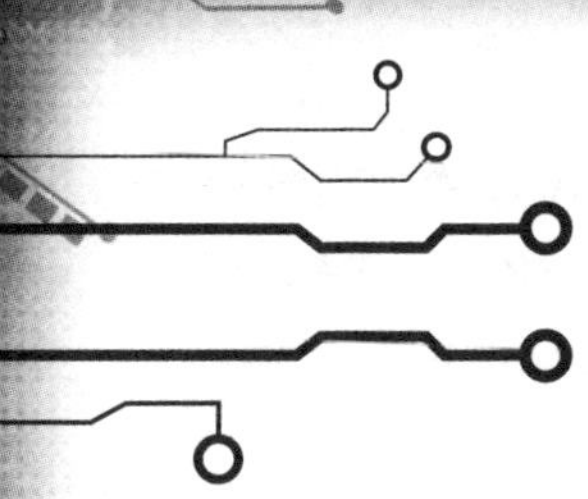

THE NET CLOSES

Since the plane crash that had destroyed Doug's house, he and his family had lived in a two-story unit painted lime green, with ivy crawling up the walls. The back fence was serious—two-metre high steel with no handholds—but someone had dumped a stepladder on the grass next to it.

Jarli climbed over the fence and pulled the stepladder over behind him so no-one else could follow. Anya had stayed at the supermarket to keep watching the mystery building. Her phone number was scribbled on a scrap of paper in Jarli's pocket, so they could communicate using Doug's phone.

No security lights clicked on. No-one yelled. The lights in the house were dark, which seemed like a good sign at first—except shouldn't Doug's family be having dinner?

Jarli crept across the stepping stones, wading through the overgrown backyard to the door. There was a lock on the screen door, and two more locks on the wooden door behind it. Jarli was just wondering if he should knock, when the wooden door opened.

'Hi,' Doug said. 'My parents went out for dinner. I told them I wasn't feeling up to it.'

Jarli swallowed. 'Have they, uh, seen the news?'

'They hadn't when they left. They might have by now, though.' Doug unlocked the screen door. 'Come in.'

Jarli did. He followed Doug through the laundry to the kitchen, the dining room, the lounge room and then the stairs. When the Federal Police moved Doug's family to Kelton, they hadn't been allowed to take much stuff with them. And the few possessions they had brought were destroyed when a plane hit their new house. The result was a lot of empty rooms. No pictures on the walls, no movies on the shelves, only one frying pan in the kitchen. Jarli wondered if that was the reason that the garden was so overgrown. Doug's parents had learned not to get too attached.

Doug seemed to have gone the other way. He had wallpapered his whole room with posters of musicians and video games. The shelves were stacked with second-hand books. Doug couldn't have read many of those books in the time he'd been here, and Jarli didn't think he had played many of the games or listened to the musicians either. Maybe having an identity was important, even if it wasn't your own.

'So,' Doug said. He shifted a screwdriver and the broken pieces of Sir Ramington to make some room on the bed, and then he sat down. 'What the heck happened?'

Jarli sat on the swivel-chair opposite and told Doug everything. The first run-in with the imposter, the golf cart chase across town, and the impostor's mysterious disappearance in the alley next to the library. Plowman's theory that someone was using *Truth Premium* to get away with crimes. The minister's anger after the press conference. The note on Jarli's bed, the smashed vase, the unconscious body, the mystery woman. Doug listened, eyes wide.

'You swear you're not having me on?' he asked, finally.

'Check your app,' Jarli said.

'My phone is off,' Doug said. 'I didn't want it to recognise your voice and alert the cops that you were here.'

Jarli squirmed. He had known that *Truth Premium* could identify people by their voice prints. He should have realised that it would be easy for the police to set up an alert for his voice. 'You reckon the cops are listening?'

'You can't be too careful,' Doug said darkly.

Jarli stared at some of the posters on the wall without really seeing them. 'You think someone is framing me?' he said.

Doug nodded vigorously. 'Did you see Dana Reynolds on the news?'

Jarli winced. 'Only the first little bit of it. I can't believe she's throwing me under the bus.'

'I'm not sure she is,' Doug said. 'She raised lots of questions about the weapon and the motive. Every other journalist is making you sound like a psychopath, but she was highlighting all the clues that suggest you might not have done it.'

'*Might* not?' Jarli objected.

'In the eyes of the public. Anyway, she said that police had refused to identify key witnesses. Meaning that someone is saying they saw you attack Lindsay. So that must be the person framing you, right?'

'Right,' Jarli said slowly. 'So if we can identify those witnesses, we'll know who the real culprit is?'

'I bet it's Viper,' Doug said.

Jarli shuddered. 'Not necessarily,' he said hopefully.

'You think there's more than one criminal mastermind in this tiny town?'

'I can't see why Viper would want to attack the defence minister.'

'We never know why he does anything. Maybe

once we know who he is, the reasons will become obvious.'

'Maybe.' Jarli rubbed his eyes. 'How long do you think I can stay here?'

'Mum and Dad both work during the day, so you can shower and eat while they're out. The weekend might be trickier. I could try to talk them into taking me to the coast, I suppose. Pretend I need to recover from the defeat at the Robattle.'

So much had happened that Jarli had forgotten all about the disaster at Kelton Town Hall. 'Thanks. Have you talked to Rebecca?'

Doug sighed. 'Not since yesterday. I think I'm dead to her. *Persona non grata*.'

'Sorry,' Jarli said.

Doug shrugged gloomily. 'It's OK. I can see why she's mad. I just wish she could see my side, too.'

Someone knocked at the front door.

'I'll see who that is,' Doug said. 'Stay quiet.'

He disappeared down the stairs.

'Wait,' Jarli hissed. But Doug was already out of earshot.

Jarli risked a peek out the window. It overlooked the backyard. He couldn't see who was on the front porch. But the trees were flickering blue and red, from lights somewhere nearby.

Jarli hurried back to the closed bedroom door

and listened. He heard Doug open the front door, and say. 'Oh. Uh, hi. What can I—hey!'

Hurried footsteps. A lot of them. Low voices.

'Check upstairs,' said a voice. DETECTIVE ARNO. She had found him!

Desperately, Jarli searched the room. He needed to hide, fast. There was just enough room under the bed, but they would check there. Jarli pulled open the wardrobe. Barely enough room to squeeze in, and not enough clothes to hide behind.

The stairs creaked. Someone was coming up. Two or three people.

The window! Jarli ran back over to it. It was locked, but not with a key. He twisted the latch, swung the frame outwards into the cold air and leaned over the overgrown garden.

It would be a long drop. Could he do it silently? Could he do it without breaking his legs?

And then it was too late. The bedroom door burst open. A torch shone on Jarli's face.

'I got him!' Arno yelled.

Jarli threw himself out the window. The wind ripped at his hair and sucked the air out of his lungs as he plummeted. He narrowly missed one of the paving stones and crashed down into a garden bed, smashing a neglected rosemary bush. He staggered to his feet and started running towards the back fence.

A police officer appeared at the top of the fence, pointing a torch at Jarli's face. 'Freeze!'

Jarli turned to run the other way, but another cop was sprinting around the side of the house. He was cornered.

Arno landed in the garden bed much more nimbly than Jarli had. Before Jarli could back away, she darted forwards and wrestled him to the ground.

'Don't shoot!' she told the other officers. 'I got him.'

Jarli found himself facedown in the dirt, his arms held behind his back.

'You didn't even draw your side-arm,' one of the cops was saying.

'I'm not gonna shoot a kid,' Arno said. 'No matter what they say he did.'

'Orders recommended lethal force. The higher-ups will wonder why—'

'Grow a spine, will you?'

Jarli went limp, letting Arno tie the flexicuffs around his wrists. It was over.

INMATE A7

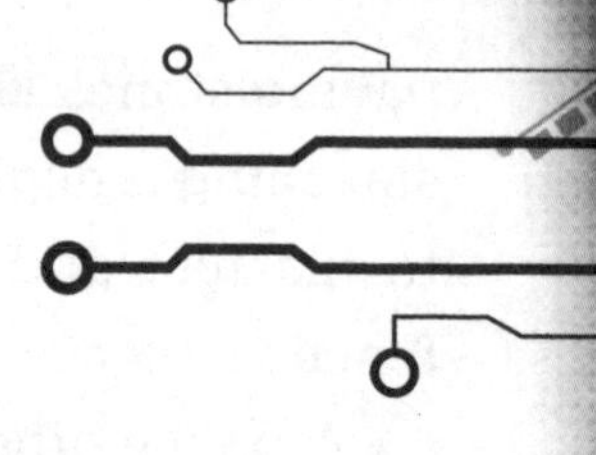

It wasn't until the police strapped Jarli to the stretcher that he realised where they were taking him.

He could wiggle his toes and fingers, but not much else. The nylon straps crushed his chest as the truck trundled through Kelton.

He struggled, but couldn't loosen his bonds. A rising tide of panic threatened to drown him. He tried to scream 'Help!' but the word came out in a choked whisper. He couldn't get enough air into his lungs.

Through the steel mesh that covered the truck's windows, he saw a familiar landmark. The library. And then, next to it, the building with no doors.

The truck turned, making Jarli feel sick. He couldn't move his arms to brace himself. If the stretcher toppled over, there would be nothing he could do to avoid being pulped by the wall.

Brakes squeaked. The truck stopped. Doors opened and slammed. Footsteps around the outside.

Locks clunked, and the back doors of the truck squeaked open.

Jarli could only look straight up, so he didn't see the driver. But he felt someone grab the stretcher and drag it out of the truck. He felt the legs unfold beneath it, and the wheels hit the ground. Then he had a brief glimpse of the star-filled sky before the stretcher rolled into the rear loading dock of the bank.

The ceiling was bare concrete, punctuated by humming fluorescent lights. The stretcher stopped next to a steel door and a keypad. The police officer entered a code and swiped a card. The door buzzed. The officer heaved it open and pushed Jarli through.

Soon the stretcher was rolling down a ramp, which tilted Jarli upside down. The blood rushed to his head. Anya had been right—there was a tunnel under the street . . . leading to the mystery building. Jarli felt sick with fear.

'What is this place?' he demanded.

The officer didn't respond. He was a middle-aged man with a greying beard and hooded eyes. From this angle, Jarli could see straight up his hairy nose.

'This isn't right,' he said. 'Do my parents know where I am?'

No reaction. When Jarli looked closer, he saw that the officer was wearing earplugs.

Jarli watched the ceiling as several CCTV cameras scrolled by. There was another set of doors—*beep, boom*—and then a big lift with another camera in it.

While laying on his back, Jarli found it impossible to tell if the lift was moving up or down. After a minute it halted, rattling the legs of the stretcher.

The driver pushed Jarli out of the lift, through yet another set of locked doors, along a corridor and then into a small room with concrete walls. He stepped away from the stretcher, out of Jarli's sight.

'Inmate A7 is in interview room three,' he said.

'Get me out of here!' Jarli demanded. 'Let me out!'

There was no response. Soon Jarli realised that the man was already gone.

Jarli wriggled and squirmed, but he couldn't loosen the straps. The claustrophobia went from worrying to frightening to painful, like ants crawling all over his skin.

The door of the cell opened, and light fell across him.

'Jarli,' Detective Arno said.

Jarli was too desperate to be angry. 'Get me off this thing!'

'Certainly.' Arno popped open some buckles, loosening the straps. Jarli rolled off the bed and hit the concrete floor, gasping.

'Sorry,' Arno said. 'The protocols for entering

this building are very strict.'

The room had a metal table, two chairs bolted to the floor, and a camera on the ceiling. Nothing else.

'Where am I?'

'The Jasper List Centre,' Arno said. 'A secret juvenile detention facility for suspects who are too dangerous to mix with the general population.'

'I'm not dangerous,' Jarli said.

'Aren't you? Witnesses saw you enter Lindsay's hotel room with a knife. They—'

'That's not true. Did you check the hotel cameras?'

'The witness claimed you concealed the knife until your back was to the security cameras. But there's footage of you pushing open the door, and we have your fingerprints from the hotel database. They're all over Lindsay's room.'

'When I called the police, the woman on the phone asked me if I was alone,' Jarli said, trying to sound calm. 'I had to search the room.'

'Your prints were also on the murder—' Arno checked herself. 'The *attempted* murder weapon. Lucky for you, Lindsay had a motorcycle accident a few years ago. There's a steel plate in his head. Otherwise his skull would have caved in, and you'd be on even more serious charges.'

Jarli remembered picking up one of the shards of the vase. 'I didn't—'

'And that's not to mention these.' Arno spread some photographs across the table. They showed Jarli in Lindsay's hotel room, standing over his body. The photos looked like they had been taken from the opposite building. Jarli remembered the flash from the rooftop. The mystery woman had been taking pictures—and she had given them to the police.

'Who gave you these?' Jarli asked.

'That's not your concern. What counts is what they show.'

'You already know I was in the hotel room. I called you guys from there.'

'You did. But you neglected to mention this, which was on Lindsay's bed.' Arno put something else on the table. A sheet of paper, sealed in a plastic bag. A letter. It looked just like the one Jarli had found in his room. Same font, same size, same margins. But the text was different.

> Listen up, Lindsay.
>
> I know what you did. You and Fisher. But I'll keep my mouth shut. For a price. I'll be in touch.
>
> Jarli

Jarli stared at the words, his eyes growing wider and wider.

'I didn't write any of that,' he said finally.

'Your fingerprints were on the envelope,' Arno said.

Jarli remembered the envelope in his own room. Unsealed. Where had he left it? 'Wait—'

'Let me tell you what I think happened. Lindsay and Fisher had done something illegal. Perhaps it had to do with the false intelligence that messed up the raid on that village, or maybe it was something else. Anyway, they had a falling out. Lindsay tried to kill Fisher in the hotel lobby—'

Jarli was getting frustrated. 'I told you yesterday, that wasn't the real Lindsay!'

'The guy in the coma is certainly the real Lindsay,' Arno said. 'Fingerprints, retinal scan, DNA—it's him. And you'd met both Lindsay and Fisher. You'd had the chance to use your app on each of them. You figured out what they had done and decided to blackmail Lindsay. You sent him a note. He summoned you to his hotel room—'

'I'm being framed,' Jarli said.

'In the argument, you picked up a vase—'

'That's not true! None of that happened!'

'Then what *did* happen, Jarli?'

Jarli stared helplessly down at the note. He knew

someone was trying to set him up, but he didn't know who or why.

'I want to help you,' Arno said. 'Don't you get that? Just tell me what you know, and I can get you out of here.'

'I'm telling you the truth!'

'The Department of Defence circulated a statement saying you were armed and dangerous. They didn't want you caught, they wanted you shot. Whatever you know about Fisher, *they know you know it*.'

'I don't know anything about Fisher!' Jarli shouted. 'This is all lies!'

Arno leaned back in her chair, running her tongue over her teeth.

'I bet your app says I'm telling the truth,' Jarli said.

'You made the app,' Arno pointed out.

'I want a lawyer.'

'You're not going to get one. This isn't a normal assault charge. The Minister for Defence and the Assistant Minister for Defence were both in the building, so counter-terrorism laws apply.' Arno leaned over the table. 'No lawyer. No phone calls. No-one knows where you are. You're staying here until you start cooperating.'

'Someone's setting me up.'

'Who?'

Jarli had no answer.

'OK,' Arno said finally. 'Have it your way.'

She walked over to the door and pushed a button on the intercom.

'Take him to his cell,' she said. 'See how he likes it in there.'

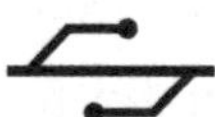

The cell was about two metres by three, with a barred door. Jarli sat down on the bed—a thin rectangle of latex on a slab of concrete. No pillow. There was nothing else in the room other than a steel toilet, a sink and a mirror. The mirror was plastic, scratched and blurry. It was too dark to see anything beyond the bars. He may as well have been in outer space.

Jarli was wearing a coarse yellow prison jumpsuit. The guards hadn't given him any pyjamas, and they had taken his other clothes away. He lay down on the bed and felt tears stinging the corners of his eyes. His chin began to quiver.

Keep it together, he told himself. *Bess wouldn't freak out. Nor would Anya. Or Doug.*

But the thought of his friends, so far away, pushed him over the limit. The tears flooded down his cheeks.

ESCAPE ATTEMPT

A bell rang. A small, old-fashioned bell, the kind an aristocrat might have used to summon a butler.

Jarli opened his eyes and panicked. Where was he? What was going on?

Oh yeah. As a light flickered on in the distant ceiling, Jarli took in the concrete cell. It didn't look any better in the daytime. He had hoped this was a nightmare. It certainly seemed too horrible to be real.

He sat up, wincing. He had slept for just long enough to make his neck stiff.

'Head count,' a voice yelled.

Jarli stood up and cautiously approached the bars. Daylight fell across the hall from the skylight high above. Now Jarli could see the other prisoners in their cells, all dressed in the same yellow jumpsuits. There were fourteen of them, a mix of boys and girls, aged between twelve and eighteen. Most lay on their beds, but a couple were hunched over their sinks, drinking from the taps. Some were standing near the bars, watching the rest of the hall, or pretending not to. It was like a human zoo.

A small woman with cat's eye glasses walked around the room, checking that every cell was occupied. Then she yelled, 'Breakfast,' and pushed a green button on the wall.

Locks clanked all around the hall. The other prisoners all pushed their cell doors open. Jarli copied, and cautiously walked out into the hall.

A yellow line was painted on the concrete. The other prisoners queued up along it, chatting.

'Move it, Pinkie,' said a boy with dreadlocks and a scarred eyebrow.

A larger kid with a shaved head blushed. 'Hey! My name isn't Pinkie.'

'Your middle name is.'

'Who told you that?' the other kid demanded.

'Sherlock always knows,' said a girl with pinched features and curly black hair.

'Check it out.' The dreadlocked boy pointed at Jarli. 'New kid.'

Everyone turned to stare. Jarli's face grew hot.

'Quiet, all of you,' the woman snapped. She counted everyone a second time. Then she pointed to the door. 'Forward march.'

CRACKED SCREEN

'He called you?' Bess said. 'Why didn't he call me?'

She was standing in the laundry at Jarli's house, leaning against the washing machine. Her crutches were propped up against a tarpaulin which, when she'd checked under it, concealed a mountain of dirty clothes.

'You're missing the point,' Doug said, his voice thin in the phone speaker.

'Jarli and I have been friends our whole lives. You breezed into town just last week—'

'I've been here more than a year.'

'Whatever.' A year was a week in Kelton time. You weren't considered local if you'd only been born here—you needed at least two generations of Kelton ancestors.

'Will you listen to me? Jarli's been arrested.'

'Arrested? When?' Bess kept her voice down. She had just escaped from the lounge room, where Jarli's mum and Kirstie were sitting on the couch like dolls, staring at the TV news with red-rimmed eyes, too exhausted to cry any more. Bess had made them cups of tea, which were growing cold on the coffee table. Glen, Jarli's dad, had disappeared into his bedroom and shut the door. *Rather than hassling the police,* Bess thought, *or comforting his family, or doing something useful.* He'd been acting WEIRD all day, but this was a new low.

'Last night,' Doug was saying. 'The police took him from my house. But I don't—'

'He went to your house?' *Why not* my *house?* Bess thought.

'But I don't know where he's gone since then,' Doug continued. 'I've been to the police station, and he wasn't there. So I went to the hospital—'

'The hospital?' Bess's heart skipped a beat. 'Why would he be at the hospital?'

'You know. In case, uh . . .'

'What are you not telling me?'

'Look, he jumped out my bedroom window, OK? When the police showed up.'

The floor seemed to shift under Bess. She found herself tilting. She tried to right herself, but as usual, her legs had other ideas. She toppled sideways and splashed down into the tarp, flailing.

'Bess?' Her phone was on the floor. The screen had cracked. 'Bess!'

Bess wriggled out of the tarp, crawled over and

picked up the phone. 'Did you see him land?'

'He can't have been badly hurt, because he wasn't in the hospital. I asked at the front desk, and they said they couldn't tell me about any specific patients, but no-one had come in all night. So we just have to figure out where he is.'

'If the police took him, at least Viper doesn't have him,' Bess said.

Doug didn't reply.

Too late, Bess remembered Doug's last run-in with Viper. A corrupt police officer had been working for the crime lord and had taken Doug and Jarli prisoner.

'I didn't actually see the police arrest him,' Doug said finally. 'The house was surrounded, and I saw a police van drive away, but I guess I don't know for certain he was inside.'

'How high is the window?'

'Second storey.'

'Let's game this out,' Bess said. It was something she'd heard Jarli say, and it sounded good. 'If the police have him, there's nothing we can do. If Viper has him, there's probably nothing we can do. But if he managed to get away somehow, he's probably hurt because you let him fall out the window.'

'What?! That wasn't—'

'So who would Jarli turn to for help?' Bess asked.

'If he needed medical attention and couldn't go to hospital because the police would check there.'

Doug paused. 'I have no idea,' he said finally.

'That's because you're not his real best friend,' Bess said. Then she hung up on Doug and called Maria Eaton. The school nurse.

MY FRIEND'S ENEMY

Breakfast was served on a plastic tray with little compartments, like a toddler might have. One of the other prisoners had dumped the tray in front of Jarli and walked away without making eye contact. There was a bread roll, so hard and stale it could potentially be used as a weapon. A mixture of rice and baked beans, still frozen in the centre. And an apple which looked OK, but one bite proved it had a spongy, floury texture. The tastiest component of the meal was the water, served in a plastic cup with a peel-off lid.

'Just imagine you're an astronaut.' A girl sat down next to Jarli. 'That's what I do. It makes the food seem nutritious in a space-age kind of way, rather than just . . . cheap.'

Jarli nodded cautiously. 'I'm Jarli.'

'Lilah.' The girl had ash-blonde hair, cut short, and eyebrows so pale they disappeared into her skin. She sat with her back perfectly straight, like a yoga teacher.

The dining hall had six plastic tables bolted to the floor, with two or three kids sitting around each one, chatting. The food had come out of a hole in the wall, too small for a person to fit through.

Jarli poked the apple. He had been starving—he hadn't eaten since breakfast yesterday—but now he had completely lost his appetite.

'You should eat,' Lilah said. 'Trust me. You need mental energy to survive this place.'

Someone else sat down opposite Jarli. A girl with freckles and a dimpled chin. 'Hi,' she said. 'You gonna eat that? What's the news from outside? I'm Bailey, by the way.'

Jarli shook her hand. 'Jarli,' he said.

It was oddly refreshing that no-one knew who he was. Jarli and his family had lived in Kelton forever. These kids must be mostly from out of town.

Bailey walked her fingers towards Jarli's tray.

Jarli took the bread roll and the water, but gave her the rest. 'Go nuts,' he said.

Bailey attacked the meal with bizarre appreciation.

'So what's going on out there?' she said, in between bites. 'You got flying cars yet?'

Jarli's eyes widened. 'How long have you been locked up here?'

Bailey's mouth was full, but she smiled and held up four fingers.

'Four years?' Jarli gasped. That wouldn't have sounded like a long prison sentence yesterday. But after a few hours in this place, the thought of spending years in here was already unbearable.

'Four months,' Lilah corrected. 'I've been here for six, which is about as long as anybody. Throwaway wasn't a prison before that, I don't think.'

'Throwaway?'

'It's what we call this place. You know, like *Throw away the key*.'

'What did you, uh . . . '

Lilah's gaze hardened. 'Nothing. I'm here because of that stupid app.'

A sinking feeling filled Jarli's chest. 'Uh, what app?'

'The lie-detector app. See, we're all here because we've been exposed to classified information.' Lilah started pointing at the other kids, one by one. 'Cassie is here because she was making a skating video and *apparently* she caught a spy meeting his handler in the background. Jerome was browsing a forum and a post from a whistleblower popped up. He saw a heap of state secrets before the post was taken down. Nic got a text message that was sent to the wrong number, with stuff in it about a raid in Malburse. Hailey was delivering a pizza to a government building. She got buzzed up to the wrong floor and walked into a meeting.' Lilah sipped her water. 'And me? I was on a school trip to parliament house, and I went looking for the bathroom. Walked through the wrong door. Next thing I know, I'm in here. As for Bailey, well, she actually hacked into the Defence Department's network. For fun.'

Bailey's mouth was still full. She grinned.

'What does any of this have to do with . . . that app you mentioned?' Jarli asked.

'Leaks aren't new,' Lilah said. 'In the old days, they would have made us all sign something. A non-disclosure agreement, saying that if we told anyone what we'd seen, we'd wind up in jail. But that app makes it basically impossible to keep a secret. Anyone could use it on us to figure out what we know. So locking us up became the government's first resort, not the last. No phones in here. No contact with the outside world. No-one even knows we're here. Threat neutralised.'

'Wow,' Jarli said. 'How long are they going to keep you here?'

'Until what I know doesn't matter anymore,' Lilah said bleakly. 'Forever, maybe.'

'Is that legal?'

'Gee, that never occurred to any of us. Nic's mum is a lawyer. Hey, Nic!' Lilah called. 'New kid wants to know if this is legal.'

Nic—a boy with black hair hanging over his eyes, and a slight stoop—spoke without looking up from his breakfast. 'Persons who pose an imminent risk to national security can be detained indefinitely without charge.'

'There you go,' Lilah told Jarli. 'So what did *you* see?'

Jarli stared down at old scratches in the tabletop. 'Nothing,' he said.

'Good behaviour won't get you far in this place.'

'I mean it. I didn't see anything and I don't know anything.'

Lilah's voice softened. 'Sorry,' she said. 'Must be terrible, not even knowing why you're here.'

Jarli reached for his water, but it was gone. He looked at Bailey, but she hadn't taken it.

'Hey,' said a voice from behind him.

Jarli turned around. The kid with the dreadlocks was behind him, holding the half-empty cup. *How did he get that without me noticing?* Jarli wondered.

'That's Sherlock,' Lilah said. 'He's just showing off. Fastest hands you ever saw—or didn't see. He wound up here after pickpocketing a guy who turned out to be the minister for defence. Sherlock, give the new kid back his water.'

Sherlock didn't. 'You're Jarli Durras,' he said, not smiling.

Jarli felt the blood drain from his face. 'Uh, yeah. Hi,' he said.

'You're here for attempted murder,' Sherlock continued. 'And you're the one who made the app.'

All the conversations in the room fell silent.

'That's true,' Jarli admitted.

Suddenly Sherlock was holding a bread roll instead of the water. It had come from Jarli's tray—he could see the dents his teeth had left in the rock-hard crust.

'It's not my fault you're here,' Jarli said, to the whole room

No-one said anything. The expressions ranged from fury to dark glee—delight that the inventor of the app was LOCKED UP in here with them.

Sherlock crushed the bread roll in one of his huge hands. Then he tipped the crumbs onto Jarli's plate.

'Watch your back,' he said. Then he turned and walked away.

BUZZ. CLANK.

There was no clock in Jarli's cell. Maybe it had been deemed cruel to put clocks in prisons. Jarli could imagine how it might feel, watching your life tick away. But not knowing the time was nearly as bad.

He could see a few prisoners in their cells across the hall, but none of them would meet his eye—except Sherlock, who leered at him with an intensity Jarli found hard to take. The light bulb in Sherlock's cell was dead, making him a shadowy figure.

Jarli could hear hushed conversations between prisoners in other cells, but couldn't make out the words. Soon he was convinced they were all talking about him.

Jarli paced around his cell. In the daylight he could see a few things he'd missed last night. A gossip magazine from about fifteen years ago. A bible. A flannel in the sink. A toothbrush. No toothpaste. The handle of the toothbrush was rubber—too bendy to use as any kind of tool. Too bendy to use as an effective toothbrush, either.

A guard pushed a trolley through the hall. The bottom shelf was loaded with books and the top was piled high with yellow jumpsuits. The guard stopped at each cell so the inmates could reach through the bars to take a book and a clean jumpsuit. Dirty ones were thrown into the canvas bag at the front of the trolley. By the time the guard got to Jarli's cell, most of the good books were gone—or maybe there hadn't been much good stuff to begin with. It was all history books, romance novels and job application guides.

Jarli took a book anyway: *The History of Mongolia, Volume Two*. It was a heavy hardcover. If the other prisoners attacked him, maybe he could use it as a weapon.

The guard quietly tapped a coin on one of the cell bars, getting Jarli's attention. Jarli looked at his face.

It wasn't a remarkable face. Pockmarked skin with fading scars. Greying hair under a dark blue cap. But Jarli recognised him. It was Lindsay—or rather, it was the man who had pretended to be Lindsay. The one who had attacked Jarli and tried to kill the defence minister.

Jarli scrambled away from the bars, suddenly terrified. Not-Lindsay had shaved off his moustache, taken out the coloured contact lenses and put on thick glasses, but Jarli was sure it was him. His name badge read: **HORSHAM.**

Horsham raised a finger to his lips, warning Jarli to be quiet. Then he held out a folded piece of paper with a gloved hand.

Jarli didn't take it. He didn't even want to approach the bars.

Horsham stood as still as a statue. Jarli didn't move either. They stared at one another for a long moment.

Then Horsham reached through the bars and dropped the piece of paper. It fluttered to the ground like a butterfly. Horsham pushed the trolley away.

Jarli took a deep, shaky breath. Did Horsham really work here, or had he stolen yet another identity? In either case, why?

There was only one way to find out. Jarli picked up the note.

I CAN GET YOU OUT OF HERE IF YOU TELL ME WHAT YOU KNOW.

YOU HAVE UNTIL MIDNIGHT TO DECIDE.

—VIPER

'Durras,' Niyoko shouted. 'Kitchen duty.'

Niyoko was one of the guards—a small woman with cat's eye glasses and a voice as rough as a screeching bird. She unlocked Jarli's cell and waited for him to shuffle out. Then she directed him out of the hall and up a narrow concrete corridor, following a few steps behind.

Jarli's thoughts had been going around in circles ever since this morning. At lunch, everyone had avoided him, but Jarli had barely noticed. All he could think about was the note from Horsham. It was Viper who had wanted to kill the defence minister, and now someone working for Viper—unless Horsham *was* Viper—was here. Viper, like Arno, assumed Jarli was in prison because he had information the defence minister wanted to conceal. He had offered to release Jarli in exchange for the information.

Jarli still had no idea what this information was, though. In fact, he was starting to think it didn't exist. Which meant Arno and Viper were both wrong about who had put him here and why.

But this realisation didn't give Jarli a way out.

Niyoko unlocked a steel door and pushed Jarli through.

'Kitchen's here,' Niyoko said. 'The other inmate knows where everything is. Ask him for help if you need it.'

Jarli found himself in a grim kitchen. No ovens, no stovetops, no microwave. There were three steam kettles—gigantic tubs with transparent lids. Each one had a canoe paddle propped up next to it, for stirring. Opposite the steam kettles was a long bench, made of stainless steel, with a hole cut into it for garbage. A coiled hose hung from the wall, ready to spray everything clean.

At the other end of the kitchen was Sherlock, sharpening a KNIFE.

Jarli swallowed. 'I worked it out,' he said.

Sherlock inspected the blade. 'Worked what out?'

'You're Dana Reynolds's other source,' Jarli said. 'Aren't you?'

Sherlock didn't answer. But Jarli knew he was right. Reynolds had known more about this prison than Anya had told her—she had someone on the inside. And Sherlock had known about the attempted murder charge. He had someone on the *outside*.

'You stole a phone from somebody,' Jarli said. 'Right?'

There was a pause, and then Sherlock smiled. 'From one of the guards,' he said. 'Picked his pocket the first day I was here. They searched every cell, couldn't find it. Eventually he assumed he'd lost it somewhere else. How do you know Dana Reynolds?'

'I owe her an interview,' Jarli said. 'How come the phone is still connected to the network? Wait—did you spoof the SIM card?'

Sherlock winked, and turned to the bench. 'Gotta hand it to you, new guy,' he said, as he started to slice an onion with the huge knife. 'You're quick.'

'How do you keep it charged?'

'That's why the light in my cell doesn't work,' Sherlock said. 'I had to do some rewiring.'

Jarli was impressed. Not even Doug could have done that—although he guessed Sherlock had more time on his hands.

'Do you have the phone on you right now?'

Sherlock didn't reply.

'With my app installed?' Jarli pressed.

Still Sherlock said nothing, but Jarli guessed he did.

'Well, listen up,' Jarli said. 'I didn't try to kill anybody. Someone is framing me.'

Sherlock turned his back on the surveillance camera in the corner, and pulled a phone out of his pocket. 'Huh.'

'See?' Jarli said. 'Now can you put down the big knife? It's making me nervous.'

Sherlock chuckled. 'Sorry. You won't find any

small knives in this kitchen. Too easy to steal. Even the potato peelers are as long as your arm.' He slid a can-opener and a giant can marked **3KG TOMATOES CRUSHED** across the bench to Jarli. 'Open this and tip it into steam kettle number two, will you?'

Jarli exhaled and started working the can-opener around the edge of the tin. 'I'm sorry my app got you locked up,' he said.

Sherlock dumped the onion slices into one of the steam kettles. They hissed, almost drowning out his voice. 'It's not really your fault. I'm sorry I threatened you. I was just mad.'

After such a disappointing breakfast and lunch, the smell of the onions made Jarli's stomach gurgle.

'Feels strange,' Sherlock said. 'Meeting someone else who knows what's happening outside. The others don't get it.'

'You could tell them,' Jarli pointed out.

Sherlock shook his head. 'I wouldn't do that to them. Knowing is worse. For the others, it's like time stopped the moment they were locked up. Whereas I get to watch the world change without me.' His eyes were watering, but that could have just been the onions.

Jarli turned away, tipping the blood-red slop from the can into the steam kettle.

Sherlock cleared his throat. 'So why would

someone be framing you?'

'I have a theory,' Jarli said. As they cooked, he explained everything to Sherlock. All the disasters of the last few days, and all the clues he'd been putting together about who was really responsible. Sherlock's eyes grew wider and wider.

'So you think Horsham is actually Viper?' he asked when Jarli had finished.

'He could just be working for Viper,' Jarli said. 'Someone told me that Viper has burns all over his face.'

'But he can also change his face, right? With surgery, or prosthetic makeup, or whatever. That's how Horsham, or whoever he really is, pretended to be the security guy.'

'Either way, I don't know what Viper will do to me when he realises I don't have the information he wants.'

'You need to get out of here,' Sherlock said.

'Tell me about it. But this building doesn't even have a door. And the tunnel is locked at both ends.'

'You said Horsham disappeared when you and that rich guy followed him into the alley next to Throwaway.'

'What does that . . . ' Jarli trailed off, thinking. Sherlock was right. Horsham knew a secret way out of here.

'But how do I convince him to let me out, since I don't actually know anything about the defence minister?'

'I have an idea,' Sherlock said.

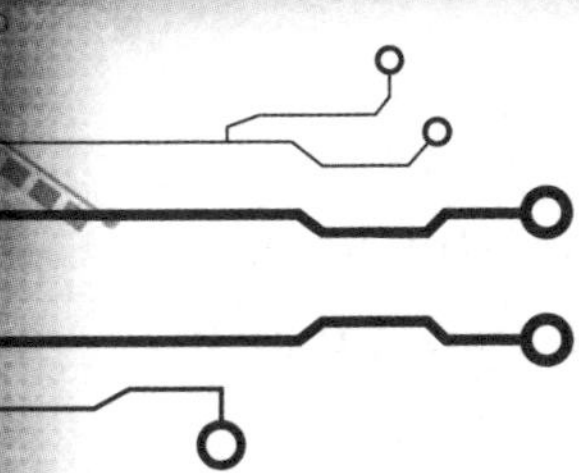

TRUST NO-ONE

'Yes?'

'It's us.'

The intercom buzzed, and the gate clicked. Doug pushed it open, and Bess hobbled after him on her crutches.

Maria Eaton lived in a small apartment block, not far from the school. The apartments were lifeless clones of painted concrete, the balconies overlooking a courtyard with a park bench under a single stunted tree.

'Glamorous,' Bess said.

Doug shrugged. 'Just like home.'

'This reminds you of home? Back in the city?'

'Yeah. We lived next door to a place like this.'

They reached the end of the courtyard, where a solid-looking door led into the apartment building. There was another intercom, this one with a camera.

Bess pushed the button for number twenty-four. 'Us again,' she said.

The door unlocked. Doug wrenched it open,

revealing Bess's least favourite thing—stairs.

'Wasn't it weird?' Bess asked, as she levered herself up onto the first step. 'Living so close to other people?'

'I think it's weird living so far away from each other,' Doug said. 'People say small towns are close—a tight-knit community, that's what they always say on the news—but it's like you people can't stand the sight of one another. Why do you need a hundred metres between houses, or a driveway a kilometre long?'

'Uh-huh. And in the city, how often did you see your neighbours? Did you even know their names?'

'I guess not. I only really had one friend.'

Bess was about halfway up the flight of stairs, struggling with the next step. Doug looked like he was about to offer to help. She hoped he didn't.

'Her name was Rebecca,' he said instead. 'We'd been best mates for our whole lives. Then she changed schools and made some new friends. I didn't like them very much.'

'What was wrong with them?'

Doug sniffed. 'Probably nothing, to be honest. I never really tried to get to know them. I guess I was just . . . offended.'

'Jealous,' Bess corrected.

'Yeah.'

She had almost reached the top of the stairs. She wobbled and gripped the rail. Doug caught her other arm and steadied it.

'Her liking them didn't mean she liked me any less,' he continued, as though nothing had happened. 'But that's not how it felt at the time.'

'I get what you're trying to do,' Bess said. 'You want me to admit that I'm just jealous of your friendship with Jarli.'

Doug reddened. 'I'm just thinking out loud.'

Bess's phone beeped, and she couldn't help but smile. 'Sure you are.'

They had reached the door to number twenty-four. Bess knocked. A shadow passed across the peephole, then two locks *ka-chunked* and the door swung open.

It was strange seeing the school nurse on a Saturday. Maria Eaton wore jeans and a singlet top. Her hair was pulled back into a loose ponytail. 'Hi,' she said. 'Come on in.'

Bess and Doug entered cautiously. The apartment was as small and lifeless on the inside as the outside. It looked like Eaton lived alone and rarely had guests. There was a lone wooden chair at the dining table. Instead of a couch in front of the TV, there was a thin meditation cushion on the floor. The books on the shelves had numbers on the spines rather than titles. Diaries, not novels. A single manila folder lay closed on the kitchen bench.

'Thanks for, uh, having us,' Doug said.

'No problem. You want something to drink?'

'Sure. What do you have?' Bess asked.

'Water,' Eaton said.

There was a pause. 'Actually, no thank you,' Bess said. 'I'm good.'

'OK.'

Eaton sat on the kitchen bench, leaving the chair for Bess. Doug sat awkwardly on the cushion.

'As I told you on the phone,' Eaton said, 'Jarli isn't here.'

'You also said you had an idea where he might be,' Bess said.

'I do. Turn your phones off.'

Bess did, but Doug hesitated. 'So you can lie to us?'

Eaton's smile didn't reach her eyes. 'Smart boy. Trust no-one.' She cleared her throat. 'I can't tell you everything,' she said. 'But everything I do tell you will be the truth.'

Doug's phone didn't beep.

'Satisfied?' Eaton asked.

Doug nodded, and turned off his phone.

'Alright,' Eaton said. 'You know that I used to be in the military, yes?'

'An army doctor, right?' Bess said.

'Right. I'm not going to tell you anything classified. But hypothetically, let's say that the military built a secret prison for enemy combatants. Here.'

Doug's eyebrows went up. 'Here in Kelton? Why?'

'Hypothetically, because it's as far from the battlefield as possible. Let's say it wasn't used all that much until recently, when the Department of Defence started using it for domestic prisoners. Let's say that a retired army surgeon knew someone who knew someone who said that a teenage boy from Kelton was transferred to that prison last night.'

Bess's heart sank. 'So you're saying that Jarli is inside a secret military prison.'

'It would be illegal for me to say that,' Eaton said. 'You'll have to draw your own conclusions.'

There was a pause.

'Hypothetically,' Doug said, 'how would we help him?'

'I think step one would be to find out who put him there.'

'The police?' Bess said.

'From what I've seen on the news,' Eaton said carefully, 'the police arrested Jarli for attempted murder. But I've met KILLERS, and he's not one. So the question is, who is feeding the police their information?'

All three looked at each other.

'Could be anyone,' Doug said.

'Let me put it another way,' Eaton said. 'Who benefits from Jarli's incarceration?'

'Anybody who's been caught out by his app, I guess,' Bess said.

'Like for revenge?' Doug asked.

'No, I mean people who might want to discredit him. If you make Jarli look like a criminal, anyone who's been caught out by his app doesn't look so bad,' Bess said.

Eaton nodded. 'Right. So who has Jarli's app humiliated recently? Is there someone who would also have enough sway with the police to get Jarli put in a secret military prison?'

Bess's eyes widened. 'The defence minister?'

'Hypothetically,' Eaton said, 'that sounds like a smart guess.'

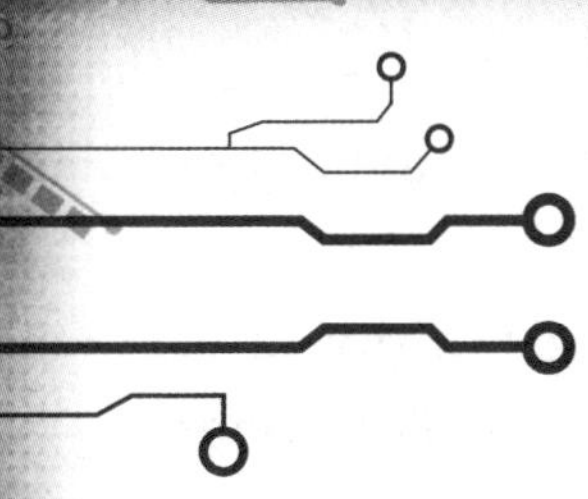

NIGHT LIGHT

Jarli prodded at his food. The steam kettles had turned everything into sludge. Even knowing that the onions had just been sliced and the rice freshly boiled, it still looked like a microwave meal.

No-one had joined him at the table. Lilah and Bailey were giving him a wide berth.

He sipped his water without really tasting it. If the plan worked, he'd be free within twenty-four hours. If it didn't work . . . well, he didn't want to think about what would happen if it didn't work.

He stood up and carried his tray over to another table. Lilah and Bailey were chewing. Neither met his eye.

If he asked for permission, they might say no. So Jarli just sat down.

'Hey,' he said.

They didn't reply.

Jarli held out his bread roll to Bailey. 'You want my leftovers?'

Bailey looked tempted, but she shook her head.

Lilah just glared at Jarli, like he'd betrayed her somehow.

'Listen,' Jarli said. 'I don't know if I'm going to make it out of here. But I think you two will. Sooner or later.'

Still both girls were silent. But suspicion was giving way to sympathy.

'So I was hoping you could remember a message for me,' Jarli said. 'Something to tell my family.'

Bailey cracked first. She gave a slight nod.

Jarli leaned in, and she flinched. Then he whispered in her ear and leaned back.

'You can remember that?' he said.

'OK,' Bailey said.

'Thanks,' Jarli said, with feeling. 'And one more thing . . .'

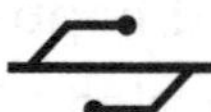

Jarli trudged back to the cell block with the rest of the prisoners. He wondered if this was really going to work. He wondered if Sherlock could be trusted. He wondered if the other inmates would speak up, ruining everything. He wondered what his family was doing right now.

He shuffled into the cell block, turned right, kept shuffling. Closed the cell door behind him.

He could see Lilah staring at him from the cell opposite, but she didn't say anything. Jarli lay down on the bunk and pulled the thin blanket over himself, leaving just the top of his head and the fingers of one hand visible. With his other hand he squeezed Sherlock's phone, hidden under his yellow jumpsuit.

A buzzer sounded, and all the cage doors locked at once.

Jarli heard Horsham walking around the cells, counting under his breath. He passed Jarli without stopping.

'All cells occupied,' Horsham said finally.

'OK,' Niyoko replied.

Jarli heard both guards leave. The main door boomed shut.

He forced himself to wait for a minute before getting ready. Making too much noise too soon would be suspicious. He counted to ten, then fifty, then a hundred. Then he pulled off the blanket and rose slowly to his feet. He crept over to the cell door and waited.

At that moment, all the lights SWITCHED OFF, leaving the cell block as dark as the inside of a coffin.

PART THREE: WAR

IT'S NOT JUST PUPIL DILATION THAT THE CAMERA IS LOOKING FOR—IT'S THE ANGLE OF THE EYES. I HEARD PEOPLE LOOK TO THE LEFT WHEN THEY'RE REMEMBERING SOMETHING REAL, AND TO THE RIGHT WHEN THEY'RE MAKING SOMETHING UP. THE DATA FROM THE APP DOESN'T SUPPORT THAT THEORY. BUT IT DOES SHOW THAT WHEN PEOPLE ARE LYING, THEY CLOSELY WATCH THE PERSON THEY ARE LYING TO.

—*From the documentation for* Truth, *version 3.3*

A SINGLE DROP

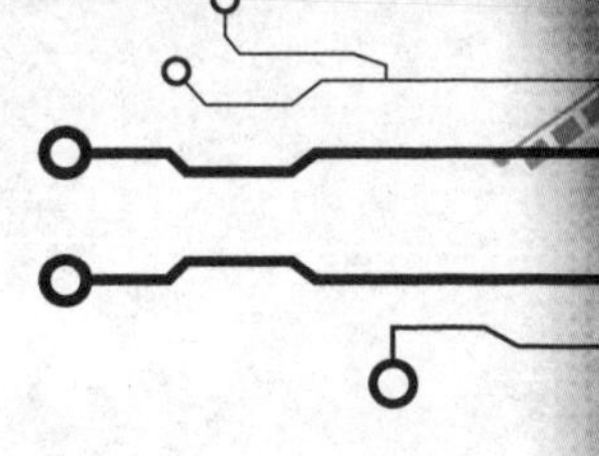

Horsham opened the cell block door as quietly as he could. Niyoko had left for the night, but not all the prisoners were asleep. He could hear a couple of them muttering about the light above the door, which was supposed to be on all night.

'What gives?'

'Bulb must have blown. Kind of a relief, actually.'

'Shut it,' a third prisoner hissed. 'Some of us are trying to sleep.'

Everything was quiet after that. Horsham heard snores from the other cells. It sounded like almost everyone was asleep. Hopefully Jarli Durras would be ready to tell everything he knew.

But if not, Viper had given Horsham a backup plan—a vial of clear fluid in his pocket. Like Throwaway itself, the poison had been developed by the military. It would shut down the inhibition centres in Jarli's brain, making him unable to keep a secret. He would voice his every thought.

Unfortunately, the brain damage would be

permanent. Jarli Durras would be unable to eat or drink or sleep. He would just talk and talk and talk until he died of exhaustion. So Horsham hoped the poison wouldn't be necessary. It would be a slow, noisy death.

The poison would break down into smaller and smaller molecules, impossible to detect in an autopsy. It would look like the bump on his head had killed Durras days after he jumped out the window.

Horsham could see almost nothing in the blackness, but he'd counted the number of steps from the door to Durras's cell. Sixteen, seventeen, eighteen.

He switched on the torch which hung from a cord around his neck. Five lumens of light. The dim blue glow wasn't enough to wake anybody. But it was enough to find the keyhole.

There was a faint click as he unlocked the door. It swung open silently. Horsham had oiled the hinges himself while Durras was at dinner.

'Durras,' he whispered. 'Your time's up. Come with me.'

The boy shuffled forward out of the darkness. Nothing in his hands. No sign that he was going to make trouble.

Horsham was too busy looking at the boy's hands. He didn't check the face. Not until the boy had already emerged from the cell, and was standing too close.

'Back off,' he said, then realised who he was talking to: Sherlock. He and Durras had swapped cells!

'Hey!' Horsham reached for his stun gun. But the holster on his hip was empty.

Sherlock pointed the stun gun at him. 'Give me your keys.'

'You don't know how to use that thing,' Horsham growled.

'You're right.' Sherlock looked curiously down at the device in his hands. 'What does this button do?'

'Wait! Don't. OK.' Horsham went to grab his keys from his belt. They were gone.

Sherlock held up the keys, grinning. 'Couldn't help myself. Hey, Jarli, catch.'

He threw the keys into another cell. Horsham heard them rattle as Durras started unlocking the door.

Other prisoners were starting to wake up.

'Who's talking?' someone complained.

'What's going on?' someone else said.

Horsham could feel himself losing control of the situation. 'You don't know who you're messing with,' he snarled. 'You think I'm gonna let you walk out of here?'

'Not just me,' Sherlock said. 'All of us.' Keeping the stun gun pointed at Horsham, he addressed the whole room. 'Listen up, everybody! This is a prison break. We're all getting out of here, right now.'

Durras was already running from cell to cell, unlocking doors.

'Are you messing with us?' Lilah demanded.

'It's true,' Durras said. 'Come on.'

'But what if we get caught?' someone asked.

'What are they gonna do?' Sherlock's voice was grim. 'Put some more years on our sentence?'

The secret exit turned out to be behind the fridge in the break room. It was a hole in the wall, just big enough to crawl through. Horsham had been happy to tell them about it, once he realised how much trouble he was in. If the prisoners didn't escape before Niyoko returned in the morning, they would inform her that he worked for Viper.

The kids left him locked in one of the cells. No phone, no keys—he could scream all he liked, but no-one would hear him.

The hole led to a narrow passage through the concrete. It was pitch black, narrow and uneven, with lots of sharp bends and sharper rocks. Even in his prison jumpsuit Jarli felt cold. He got the feeling that no heat from inside or outside ever burrowed this deep into the wall.

Eventually Jarli hit a dead end. He panicked for a moment—there was no room to turn around, he was stuck!—and then realised that two handles were bolted to the bricks. Jarli gripped the handles and pushed.

A big chunk of wall rolled outwards, and MOONLIGHT spilled into the tunnel. Jarli poked his head out, checking that there were no people outside. Then he crawled through the gap.

He found himself in the alley between the library and the prison—the same place Horsham had disappeared from. The removable chunk of wall was attached to the back of the dumpster.

'Clear,' he said.

The others scrambled out of the tunnel one by one. Lilah was staring upwards with wonder. The stars were just visible between the eaves of the two buildings.

'We should split up,' Bailey was saying. 'There aren't enough cops in this town to chase all of us.'

'Right,' Jarli said. 'But we won't get far in our prison clothes. There's a charity bin around the corner, that way. Further along the road there's a petrol station where trucks stop all the time. You might be able to stow away in the back of one.'

Some of the prisoners still looked giddy with freedom, but others were starting to look unsure, facing life on the run.

'What about you?' Sherlock asked Jarli. 'You going home?'

Jarli shook his head. He'd only be caught. 'I'm going to clear my name. Prove I was set up.'

'Good luck,' Sherlock said.

'You too.'

Jarli ran through the maze of quiet roads, staying out of the streetlights. Soon his heart was racing and his lungs burning, but he didn't dare slow down. He retraced the route that Plowman's golf cart had taken, across the train tracks, down the highway and then through the brush until he reached the fence. He climbed over and landed in the shrubbery on the other side.

A flash in the corner of his eye. Jarli turned. Someone was walking across the golf course towards him. He couldn't tell who it was at this distance, but he could see a bouncing torchlight, and a dog on a leash.

Either one of the hotel guests was taking a pet for a midnight walk, or security was here. Jarli might be OK if it was Plowman's security team, but if it was the ministerial team or the police, he was in trouble.

The person—a woman, Jarli thought—wasn't running. Just patrolling the lawns, maybe because of all the government officials staying at the resort. He didn't think she had seen him or heard him. But she would if he tried to run.

Very slowly, Jarli backed away until he was behind one of the trees. It wasn't quite thick enough to conceal him, so he crouched down in the undergrowth around it. If her torch beam touched his yellow prison jumpsuit, he was done for.

The woman walked closer and closer to Jarli's hiding place, as Jarli watched from between the leaves.

Suddenly the dog was straining at the lead. It was a Kelpie, nose twitching, ears up, tail straight out.

The woman ignored this. She jerked the leash tight. 'Come on.'

A low growl came from the back of the dog's throat, like a zipper on a tent.

Suddenly alert, the woman turned to look at the trees. There was a moment of stillness. Jarli could only hear his own heartbeat.

The dog sniffed at the edge of the shrubs. The woman slowly lifted her torch. The beam crawled across the undergrowth towards Jarli. He closed his eyes, like a little kid. *You can't see me if I can't see you.*

The woman's radio crackled. 'Emergency. K9 unit, where are you?'

The woman touched her lapel. 'On the north fence. What's the emergency?'

'A prison break in the town centre. Dozens of inmates on the loose. We need every available officer—state, federal, whatever—on scene, ASAP.'

'What prison?' the woman asked. 'There's no—'

'Are you kidding me? Get out there!'

With one last suspicious glance at the trees, the woman dragged the dog away from the undergrowth and started running back across the golf course towards the hotel. The dog followed, tongue flapping sideways as it ran.

Jarli let the air out of his lungs as he slowly stood. He hoped the prisoners had managed to get into a truck before someone raised the alarm. A guilty feeling swam around in Jarli's guts. This had been his idea—his and Sherlock's. He hoped no-one got hurt.

As he ran across the dewy grass towards the hotel, he saw headlights flick on in the distant car park. He threw himself to the ground as the twin beams of light swung across the golf course, and watched the police car drive away. Followed by another, and another, and another. Soon the only remaining vehicles looked like civilian cars.

But the ministers and visiting dignitaries wouldn't

be left unguarded for long. And if any of the hotel staff saw Jarli, they'd call the police straight away. If Jarli was going to sneak in, he would need a distraction.

And even if he could get inside, it wouldn't be enough just to confront the real criminal. He needed proof that he'd been set-up.

Jarli pulled out Sherlock's phone and called a number he knew off by heart.

Doug snorted, snuffled, and thrashed around in his blankets for a bit. Something was buzzing. Killer bees. No, his phone. An alarm. But it was still dark outside.

His Dad had told him not to sleep with the phone in his room. *Poor sleep hygiene,* he always said, with a disappointed shake of his shaggy head. But Doug always had do-not-disturb mode switched on at night. His phone wouldn't make any noise unless the same person called three times in five minutes.

Doug rubbed his eyes and grabbed the phone. He checked the time first. 02:12. He had only been asleep since midnight, after hours of tossing and turning.

The phone kept buzzing urgently. Maybe it was

Rebecca. She had sent him a message earlier in the evening, offering to help him fix Sir Ramington before she flew home. The message didn't actually say *I forgive you,* but Doug was sure it was a step in that direction.

He had already repaired the robot, but he was thinking about breaking it again so he'd have an excuse to see her.

Doug squinted at the painfully bright screen. A number he didn't recognise.

Normally he wouldn't answer a call like that. But with everything that had happened over the last couple of days . . .

He pushed the button. 'Yeah?'

'Uh, hi,' a teenage boy's voice said. 'Did you know you could save . . . fifty dollars per month on your, um, insurance?'

Doug's eyes widened. 'Jarli? Is that you?'

'Oh good, I wasn't sure if you would be alone. Listen—'

'It's two in the morning. Of course I'm alone. Where are you? No, wait.' Doug was starting to wake up now. 'Don't tell me. The police could be listening.'

There was a pause. And then:

'I guess it doesn't matter if they are,' Jarli said finally. 'One way or another, this will all be over soon.'

His words gave Doug an uneasy feeling. 'What do you mean? What's going on?'

'Listen, I need help.' Jarli explained the situation and his plan.

Doug blinked furiously, trying to clear the cobwebs of sleep from his brain. 'Slow down,' he told Jarli. 'You programmed Sir Ramington—you know that's not how his AI works. He can avoid obstacles, sort of, but only if he's already moving, or if something is moving towards him. He can't just roll in and stir up trouble, can he?'

There was a pause. 'No,' Jarli said finally. 'You're right. We'll need to reprogram him.'

'That'll take hours. Days. Unless we fit him with a remote instead? Just to get him into the building?'

'Can you do that? Quickly?'

'Maybe,' Doug said. 'But I don't own a controller we could use, and I don't have the skills to . . . ' He trailed off, thinking. 'But I know somebody who does. I'll call you back.'

He ended the call, took a deep breath, and found Rebecca's number in his contact list. He pushed the call icon.

The phone rang and rang. She probably wouldn't answer. She hadn't during the day—Doug assumed his chances were even worse now.

But suddenly he could hear her. 'Terence? It's

two in the morning.'

'Rebecca! Hi,' Doug said. 'Uh, thanks for answering.'

'I regret it already,' Rebecca said. 'I'm hanging up now.'

'Wait wait wait. Don't. Please, I need your help. Are you still in Kelton?'

A pause. 'I'm at the motel,' Rebecca admitted reluctantly.

'I need to fit Sir Ramington with a remote,' Doug said. 'Tonight. And he needs a pilot. A good one.'

'Are you serious right now?'

'Please. Actual human lives are at stake.' Doug explained the situation, stammering and tripping over his words.

Rebecca listened in silence.

'Well,' she eventually said. 'I guess you'd better tell me where you live these days.'

THE FINAL SHOWDOWN

Richie looked up.

It had been a funny sort of night. First the police were all over the place guarding against more attacks. Then they all vanished, and the concierge had heard someone say something about a prison break near the library, which made no sense since Richie had lived in Kelton all his life, and if there was a prison here he would have heard about it.

And now a robot was at the door.

It wasn't much bigger than a remote control car, but it looked like a battering ram on wheels. The metal sides were scratched and dented.

The robot bonked against the glass of the sliding doors, zoomed back, and bonked forwards again. Eventually the doors opened, and the little robot zoomed through, the wheels making happy zipping noises as they churned across the carpet.

Richie stayed still for a moment. Was this a prank? An attack? An alien invasion? It seemed safest not to move. And then he saw the twin streaks of mud trailing behind the robot on the cream carpet.

During the day, Richie would just have left the mess for someone else to find. But no-one was here right now. There was nobody else to take the blame. If Mr Plowman saw it, he'd be furious.

Richie raced out from behind the desk and chased after the robot. But the thing was fast. It swerved left and right under lounge chairs and low tables, running circles around him. It seemed to sense Richie chasing after it. Every time he stooped down to grab it, it changed direction, zooming out of reach.

Doug slapped Jarli on the back. 'Go, go!'

Jarli burst out of the bushes and sprinted across the car park towards the hotel. Doug watched as the automatic glass doors opened and he slipped through. Then he was out of sight behind one of the pillars in the lobby. From here, Doug and Rebecca couldn't see the robot or the guy from the front desk either.

'OK,' Rebecca said, stuffing her controller back into the bag. 'Autopilot is on.'

'Thanks, Rebecca,' Doug said. 'No-one else could have rigged that remote so fast. I owe you, for real.'

'I'll put it on your tab,' Rebecca said. 'How well do you know Jarli?'

Doug shrugged. 'We hang out a lot. It took a long time for us to get the robot competition-ready.'

'And the girl helping him? Anya?'

'I've only talked to her a couple of times,' Doug said, getting uncomfortable. He knew Rebecca well enough to hear her thoughts. Back home, he had been kind of a loner. Rebecca had been his only friend. But here in Kelton, he had found his tribe. Moved on.

Rebecca didn't seem jealous, though. 'Well, they seem cool,' she said. 'We should all keep in touch.'

'Yeah.' Doug cleared his throat. 'That'd be nice. If we survive.'

Rebecca put a hand on his arm. 'I'm glad you're not dead.'

'You too,' Doug said automatically, and then blushed. Rebecca stifled a laugh.

'Look, I'm sorry,' Doug said. 'I should have tried to reach out to you. Before.'

'It's OK. I'm starting to see why you didn't.' Rebecca was watching the dark windows of the hotel. 'This is serious stuff. But don't ghost me again, OK? Whatever happens, we stay friends. Deal?'

She held out her hand. Doug shook it. 'Deal.'

Richie picked up the pace, puffing as he gained ground on the robot. He leapt forward, trying to tackle it, but it darted out of the way just in time. Richie crashed down onto the muddy carpet, ruining his uniform.

Angry now, he scrambled to his feet and kept chasing the robot. It continued darting from side to side, but this time Richie had worked out how to trap it. He overturned tables and kicked over chairs as he ran, stopping the robot from escaping underneath them. Soon he had corralled it into a corner. Before it could zip away again, he stomped on it.

He had expected it to smash in a satisfying way, but it was too solid. It whirred and groaned under his polished shoe, trying to get away.

Richie picked up the robot. It weighed no more than a laptop. The wheels spun helplessly in the air. He carried it back to the front doors. They parted as he approached. Then he flung it out into the darkness, and heard it land in the car park somewhere with a crash.

When the doors closed, he locked them. Just in case the robot was intact enough to have another go. Just in case there were more of them.

He hadn't seen the boy in the prison jumpsuit sneak past.

I made it. I'm in Building B, on the 4th floor.

Jarli sent the text to Doug. Then he called Anya.

Anya answered quickly, but she sounded out of breath. The wind CRACKLED over the line. 'Jarli. Where are you?'

'I'm ready to knock on the door,' Jarli whispered. 'Where are you?'

'The third floor. In thirty seconds I will be in position.'

'Good luck,' Jarli whispered.

'You too.'

Jarli ended the call and started counting. It was the longest thirty seconds of his life.

A text came through from Doug.

You're clear. The hotel guy is cleaning the carpet. He doesn't realise anyone got past him.

Thanks. It's time to make the call.

Jarli opened a microphone app and hit *record*. Then he pocketed his phone and approached the door of Room 402. He knocked—three loud taps. Then he yelled, 'Sorry, wrong room,' and ducked out of sight below the peephole.

He waited. Long enough for a curious person to look out the peephole, seeing no-one. Long enough for her to open the door and poke her head out to get a look at the person who had just walked away.

There was a pause, giving Jarli enough time to think this wasn't going to work. Then muffled footsteps approached. The door opened, but not all the way. There was a chain.

Through the gap, Jarli saw the face of the assistant minister for defence.

'Uh, hi,' Jarli said.

Sellick's eyes widened as she saw him crouched on the floor. She tried to slam the door shut. Jarli jammed his prison boot into the gap just in time. The door thunked against his foot. He barely felt it.

Keeping pressure on the door, Sellick pulled out her phone.

'I'm a wanted fugitive,' Jarli said. 'If you call the police, they'll arrest me.'

'That's the idea,' Sellick said.

'Last time they arrested me, I didn't know who put that note in my room,' Jarli said. 'Now I do.'

Sellick hesitated. It looked like she'd already dialled, but she didn't put the phone to her ear.

'If I get arrested, I'll tell them everything,' Jarli said. 'I don't think they'd have too much trouble proving it.'

'I don't know what you're talking about,' Sellick said.

Sherlock's phone beeped in Jarli's pocket. LIE

'See?' Jarli said. 'All it takes is for someone to ask you the wrong question, and you're done.'

Sellick said nothing. Admitted nothing.

'Now you're wondering why I'm here,' Jarli said, 'instead of just telling the police what I know.'

'You're going back to jail,' Sellick said, and lifted the phone to her ear.

'My dad is sick,' Jarli said. 'He can't work, the bills are piling up. You know that already. It's how you got me to the conference in the first place.'

He had to speak carefully. He couldn't lie, or both his phone and Sellick's might go off.

'For the right price,' he continued, 'I might be willing to disappear.'

Sellick stared at him. 'You'd spend the rest of your life on the run to protect your family?'

'I would,' Jarli said, truthfully. 'If you let me in, we can discuss terms.'

Still Sellick hesitated.

'Isn't it funny?' Jarli said. 'You planted evidence to make it look like I was blackmailing someone. And now I actually am.'

Sellick unhooked the chain and opened the door. The pressure on Jarli's foot eased.

'Come in,' Sellick said.

Relieved, Jarli scrambled up and scurried inside.

Then Sellick closed the door, turned around and pointed a gun at him.

TERMINATED IMMEDIATELY

It wasn't a stun gun. It was the real kind that fired actual bullets. Sellick was aiming it right at Jarli's heart. It was as steady in her grip as a rock.

'Take the phone out of your pocket,' she said. 'Slowly.'

Jarli removed the phone from the pocket of his jumpsuit. The screen was off. He kept his thumb over the blinking light in the corner, so Sellick wouldn't realise he was recording everything she said.

'Turn it off,' she said. 'Keep the screen facing me.'

Jarli did. The screen flashed and went dark. No more recording. Jarli's heart sank.

'Now put it on the floor. Kick it over into the corner. Then move away from the door.'

Jarli obeyed, walking slowly all the way over to the window. He kept his hands up as he stood with his back to the glass.

Sellick stayed facing him, blocking the path to the door.

'I'm unarmed,' Jarli said. 'You invited me in.

Someone will hear the shot. You'll get arrested. You can't shoot me.'

'I can,' Sellick said. She put on a fake helpless voice. 'Officers, thank goodness you're here. I was just slicing an apple, and I heard a knock on the door. As soon as I opened it, he burst in—the escaped criminal, from the news! I wish I'd put the chain on. He had a gun, but I managed to knock it out of his hands. Then he grabbed the knife I'd left on the table. He charged at me with it, but I picked up the gun, and . . . and . . .'

Her lip trembled, and Jarli was amazed to see tears spring into her eyes. Then, like someone had flicked a switch, the emotion vanished from her face. She looked as cold as a lizard.

'See?' she said.

'My app will say you're lying,' Jarli said.

'*Your* app might,' Sellick said, 'but *Truth Premium* won't. And that's what the police and media use. There's a secret list of people who are always trusted by *Truth Premium*. If you pay the right amount to Viper, you can get on that list.'

Jarli felt like he was falling. Accelerating. '*Viper* made *Truth Premium?*'

Sellick smiled. 'Not just that. It was Viper who spread the word about your app in the first place. He made it go viral.'

Jarli wondered why. But now wasn't the time—he had to work out how to save his own life first. 'Lindsay knows I'm innocent,' he said. 'When he wakes up—'

'He's not going to wake up. He's about to have a bad reaction to some medication.'

'You can't kill me,' Jarli insisted. 'I've already told people about you.'

Sellick didn't look worried. 'Told them what? You don't even know what I did.'

This was true. All Jarli had was theories. If he was wrong, Sellick might shoot him.

'You wanted Fisher's job,' he said. 'So you arranged for him to be publicly humiliated. You knew about the secret prison he had been using to hide young people. You knew it was his fault that soldiers and innocent people died in a botched raid. So you tipped Dana Reynolds off about them both. You arranged for me to be there when she asked the question, to get more publicity. Making sure everyone saw him get caught in a lie.'

'None of that sounds illegal,' Sellick said. 'Goodbye, Jarli.' She raised the gun.

'But you didn't want the same thing to happen to you,' Jarli said quickly. 'So after Fisher was disgraced, you needed to discredit me. You framed me for attempted murder.'

Sellick hesitated, her finger on the TRIGGER.

'It was you, taking pictures on that rooftop,' Jarli said. 'Then you sent them to the police, making it look like I attacked Lindsay. You told them I was armed and dangerous. You put pressure on them to shoot me on sight. When that didn't work, you had me locked up in Fisher's secret prison to keep me quiet.'

'You can't prove any of this,' Sellick scoffed.

Jarli kept talking. 'Did you find Lindsay's body in the hotel room, and decide to use it? Or did you buy it from Viper, when you were paying for immunity from *Truth Premium?*'

'I don't think you've told anybody anything,' Sellick said.

'My friend Doug called the police,' Jarli said. 'Before I even knocked on your door. I knew you'd try to kill me. The police will be on their way right now.'

Sellick's eyes narrowed. 'You're lying.'

'No. I'm Truth Boy,' Jarli said. 'Remember?'

Sellick straightened her arm, levelling the gun at Jarli's face. The black hole of the barrel stared at him. It was now or never.

'I also told my friend Anya,' Jarli said. 'She's on the balcony, live-streaming this whole conversation. Did I mention my app has a lip-reading algorithm?'

Sellick's gaze shifted slightly. She squinted into the darkness beyond the window. Then her eyes widened.

'You little—' she began.

Then the door burst open.

Jarli dived into the corner of the room as Sellick spun towards the door, gun first. Three police officers swarmed into the hotel room, led by Detective Arno. Sellick opened fire—*Blam! Blam!*—but Detective Arno was already wrestling the gun out of her hands. The two shots went high, blasting holes in the ceiling. Plaster rained down. Someone screamed elsewhere in the hotel.

Jarli had curled into a ball behind the bed, covering his head with his hands. Someone grabbed his wrists, and he screamed.

'It's OK,' the police officer said, holding him still. 'It's over. It's over.'

He heard the balcony door roll open.

'We did it, Jarli!' Anya cried.

'Uh, boss,' one of the cops said to Arno. 'We got a second kid here.'

Jarli turned his head, looking under the bed. Sellick was visible on the other side, pinned to the floor by two cops.

She looked beaten. It really was over.

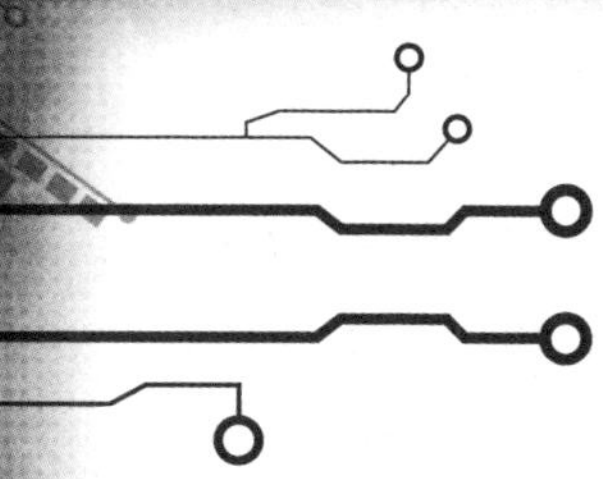

NEW FACE

'So,' Dana Reynolds said. 'How do you feel now that—'

'Stop!' the camera operator yelled, and Jarli flinched. It had been three days since he had been at gunpoint in Sellick's hotel room, but loud noises still made him jump.

'Sorry, Dana,' the camera operator said. 'We're getting too much shine off his forehead again.'

'I'm on it,' the make-up man said. He ran over and dabbed at Jarli's forehead with something spongy. This was the third time this had happened.

Reynolds had offered Jarli money, but he had turned it down, hoping to keep the interview short. Dad had found a new employer—a medical research company—so Mum had quit her second job. Everything was almost back to normal. But this shoot was taking all morning.

The makeup guy backed off.

'Recording,' said a woman near a mixing board.

'Frame,' said the camera operator.

'Action,' said the director.

'So,' Reynolds said, just like before. 'How do you feel now that Kellin Plowman, one of the country's most successful tech entrepreneurs, is taking an interest in your firewall?'

'Uh, it's so exciting,' Jarli began. 'I—'

'We'll get you to repeat the question in your answer,' the director interrupted. 'In case Dana's question doesn't make the final cut.'

Jarli swallowed. 'It's so exciting that Kellin Plowman is taking an interest in my firewall.'

'And has he made you an offer you can't refuse?'

Jarli didn't want to say the exact figure on TV. 'He's made me an offer I can't refuse,' he said obediently.

Reynolds offered him a thin smile. 'That's great, thanks—we're almost done. The prison you were held at has been closed, pending a full investigation. Thanks to public protests and a high court challenge, many of the prisoners are likely to go free. Aaron Fisher claims the Assistant Minister for Defence, Norma Sellick, was entirely responsible for the prison and had concealed its true purpose from him. Do you believe him?'

'I don't know,' Jarli said. He thought Fisher was probably lying, but he didn't want to say so on national TV. Not now that Fisher seemed likely to keep his job after all.

'Have you been invited to give evidence to the high court?' Reynolds pressed.

'I was there less than twenty-four hours. My evidence wouldn't be very useful.'

'The corrupt guard, Xander Horsham, is still missing. So is Wayne Cargo, the prisoner nicknamed Sherlock. Does that make you nervous?'

'No,' Jarli said. 'I reckon they're both long gone.'

Lindsay, the real security chief, had finally woken up from his coma. Trembling, he had described being attacked by someone wearing his face. The police were still trying to explain this. Long-lost twins was a remote possibly.

'Last question,' Reynolds said. 'After examining the email and phone records of Sellick and Horsham, police have concluded that Viper organised the attempt on Fisher's life *before* Sellick contacted him. Why do you think Viper wanted to attack the Minister for Defence?'

'I'm sorry,' Jarli said. He was still so tired. 'I have no idea.'

Later, he watched the interview on the TV. After editing, he was only on the air for seven seconds. They had edited it down to one line: 'It's so exciting that Kellin Plowman is taking an interest in my firewall.'

'Are you watching this?' Cobra asked, his feet on the coffee table as he squinted at the TV.

'I'm watching everything,' Viper said, his voice a DISTORTED RASP in the phone. 'Like always.'

Cobra rolled his eyes, and then regretted it. He was still getting used to the contact lenses which changed the colour of his irises. They stung when he looked up too high too suddenly.

'You know what I mean,' Cobra said. 'The kid's on the TV right now, bragging about how rich he's about to be when Plowman buys his new software. You sure you don't want me to kill him?'

'I definitely do not want that.'

'You told me to kill him once before.'

'And you screwed it up. Now I'm telling you to keep him alive. Is that going to be a problem?'

Cobra blew out a long stream of air from his nostrils. 'No.'

'I spent a lot of money on your new face. If we kill him now, it's all wasted.'

Cobra grunted, and shovelled some more noodles into his mouth, wishing he could eat a steak. But he wasn't allowed any chewy foods. Not until his jaw had reset properly.

'How is your face, by the way?'

Cobra touched the stitches under his jaw, mostly hidden by his beard. 'Healing,' he said.

'Does anyone suspect anything?'

'No.'

'The mother? The sister?'

'No-one.'

'Good. I don't want the kid dead,' Viper said. 'But nor do I want him to interfere with any more of my plans. Are you confident that you can keep him out of my way? Because if not—'

'Yeah, yeah. Relax, I got this.'

A key rattled in the front door.

'I have to go,' Cobra said, and ended the call.

Jarli Durras walked into the house and went straight to the kitchen. He looked over as he poured a glass of water. Saw Cobra on the couch.

'Hi, Dad,' he said.

'Hi, son,' Cobra said. 'How was school?'

'Busy,' Jarli said. 'I'm still catching up.'

Cobra smiled, stretching the skin of his new face to show his teeth. 'Just so long as you're staying out of trouble,' he said.